W9-BRN-259

Jane Porter is a rising star of Harlequin Presents®. Her exciting stories are packed full of sizzling attraction and provocative passion! Jane's feisty and courageous heroines are wonderfully matched with powerful and passionate heroes that are loved the world over!

Praise for Jane Porter:

"If you enjoy romances with alpha-heroes who'll sweep you off your feet and set your pulse pounding, you'll definitely want to read Jane Porter."
—*www.thebestreviews.com*

"Jane Porter is definitely an author to watch!"
—*www.heartratereviews.com*

"Jane Porter offers an intense, compelling story that's hard to put down!"
—*Romantic Times*

THE Galván Brides

by
Jane Porter

Look for all the titles in this sexy, Latin quartet!

In Dante's Debt #2298
Lazaro's Revenge #2304
The Latin Lover's Secret Child #2358
The Spaniard's Passion #2363

Available only from Harlequin Presents®.

Jane Porter

THE SPANIARD'S PASSION

THE Galván Brides

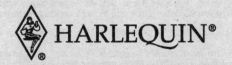

HARLEQUIN®

TORONTO • NEW YORK • LONDON
AMSTERDAM • PARIS • SYDNEY • HAMBURG
STOCKHOLM • ATHENS • TOKYO • MILAN • MADRID
PRAGUE • WARSAW • BUDAPEST • AUCKLAND

If you purchased this book without a cover you should be aware
that this book is stolen property. It was reported as "unsold and
destroyed" to the publisher, and neither the author nor the
publisher has received any payment for this "stripped book."

For my mom, Marybeth Higuera,
who taught me to love travel and adventure. I love you!
Jane

ISBN 0-373-12363-9

THE SPANIARD'S PASSION

First North American Publication 2003.

Copyright © 2003 by Jane Porter.

All rights reserved. Except for use in any review, the reproduction or
utilization of this work in whole or in part in any form by any electronic,
mechanical or other means, now known or hereafter invented, including
xerography, photocopying and recording, or in any information storage
or retrieval system, is forbidden without the written permission of the
publisher, Harlequin Enterprises Limited, 225 Duncan Mill Road,
Don Mills, Ontario, Canada M3B 3K9.

All characters in this book have no existence outside the imagination of
the author and have no relation whatsoever to anyone bearing the same
name or names. They are not even distantly inspired by any individual
known or unknown to the author, and all incidents are pure invention.

This edition published by arrangement with Harlequin Books S.A.

® and TM are trademarks of the publisher. Trademarks indicated with
® are registered in the United States Patent and Trademark Office, the
Canadian Trade Marks Office and in other countries.

Visit us at www.eHarlequin.com

Printed in U.S.A.

PROLOGUE

THE blazing sun dazzled the eyes and the steady crash of waves on the long sandy beach lulled Sophie Johnson to sleep. She snuggled deeper into her towel on the warm sand. She'd had more fun in the last ten days than she'd had...well, than she'd had...ever.

Abruptly the sand shifted and a shadow stretched over her. Sophie's stomach tensed: a knot of excitement and fear. Shading her eyes, she glanced up, knowing it was Alonso Huntsman. How could she adore someone so much when he made her this nervous?

Alonso was standing over her, dripping wet, his black hair slicked back from his face, the hard planes of his chest darkly tan from a summer spent in the sun. "You smell fantastic, Sophie. I think I'll eat you."

She tried to ignore the way her heart jumped. "It's just lotion, Lon. I'd taste disgusting."

He flashed her a wicked grin. "I'll be the judge of that."

Clive Wilkins, son of prominent banker Lord Wilkins, stirred restlessly on his towel next to Sophie. "Will you two kindly shut up?"

Alonso reached for his towel, his muscles rippling as he mopped his face dry. "Are we disturbing your sleep, old man?"

"Yes. As a matter of fact, you are," Clive retorted, burying his blond head deeper into the crook of his arm.

"Just one little taste," Lon whispered to Sophie over Clive's head, his light blue eyes glowing. He knew he was being wicked. He also knew it thrilled her.

"One taste?"

He nodded seriously. "Just one good lick."

Squirming on the inside, trying not to laugh, she picked up her bottle of suntan lotion and tossed it to him. Lon caught it with one hand. "Here you go, big boy. Enjoy."

"Oh, for God's sake!" Clive swore, sitting up. "You've just ruined a brilliant nap." He grabbed Sophie's arm, pressed her wrist to his mouth and flicked his tongue across her warm skin.

"Disgusting," Clive pronounced, tossing her arm away. He lay back down again, nestling his unshaven cheek to his arm, the blond bristles glinting gold. "She tastes like synthetics and plastic. You'd hate it, Lon. Now, will you two please shut up so I can sleep?"

"You just don't want me to taste her," Lon mocked, dropping down next to the two of them. "I think you're jealous, old man."

Clive didn't even bother to open his eyes. "Jealous of you two pathetic human beings?" His aristocratic English had never been more precise. "Of course, you big Scottish meat-head. You and the princess are the two best friends a man could ask for."

Meat-head. Princess. Sophie bit her lip, trying not to giggle, but she couldn't hold the laughter in. Once she started to laugh Lon and Clive joined in, and suddenly her eyes were burning with tears she wouldn't cry.

This was the best school holiday of her life. No, make it the best summer of her life. Clive and Lon were impossible. Incorrigible. Irredeemable. And she'd never loved anyone so much.

Nothing, she thought as she surreptitiously wiped a tear away, gazing out at the Pacific Ocean where the waves crashed against Buenaventura's white sandy beach, nothing would ever top this. Nothing would ever be as sweet; nothing would ever be as innocent.

If only time would stop and the three of them could remain together, forever, like this.

CHAPTER ONE

"How much?" Lady Sophie Wilkins asked, holding her hand up, watching the ring catch the light. The marquis cut emerald surrounded by smaller diamonds glittered in the jewelry store's bright fluorescent lighting, throwing off white sparks like fireworks exploding on New Year's Eve.

"Ten thousand pounds," the jeweler answered.

She turned her hand a little, mesmerized by the hot glow of the emerald and the brilliant blue and yellow streaks of fire in the white stones.

She heard the jewelry store door open but she couldn't tear her gaze from the glittering stone on her finger. Ten thousand pounds, she silently repeated, ten thousand pounds, knowing she'd never have anything half so beautiful again. But she couldn't keep it. She had to get to Brazil, and she still had so many bills to pay, and ten thousand pounds would settle a lot of debts.

Her silence troubled the jeweler. "I might possibly be able to do ten thousand five hundred," he said as though she'd squeezed the offer from him, "but that's my best price, Lady Wilkins. I couldn't go higher."

"Not even though you'll get twice that much tomorrow?" a deep male voice asked mockingly.

Sophie felt a shadow cross her grave. It couldn't be...

Slowly she looked up, and slowly her eyes focused. The air left her throat. She swayed a little on her feet. *"Lon?"*

"Sophie."

She couldn't look away, her hand balled into a fist and

she kept staring at him as if she'd seen a ghost. "What are you doing here?"

"Taking care of some business."

"Business?" she repeated numbly, as if it were a foreign concept, although she knew Alonso was one of the world's leading emerald exporters.

The jeweler hurriedly put away his monocle and the black velvet pad on the counter. "I didn't expect you until tomorrow, Mr. Huntsman. The stone's not even cleaned yet."

Sophie's eyes searched his face even as her fingers curled around the wedding ring still on her fourth finger.. "You're buying a stone?"

"An emerald," Lon answered.

He'd traveled halfway around the world to buy an emerald? "Must be valuable."

His eyes never left hers. "It came from my mine, so I suppose you could say it has sentimental value."

As he'd talked she'd gone hot, then cold, and now she tugged her wedding ring from her finger and handed it to the jeweler. "I accept your offer."

The jeweler nodded his head, pocketing the ring Clive had given her nearly six years ago. "Will you take a check, Lady Wilkins?"

"Yes." Her throat seemed to be squeezing closed. "Thank you." The jeweler moved across the shop and chilled, Sophie began to button her long wool coat.

"You're selling your wedding ring?" Lon asked, black lashes lowered, concealing his expression.

"It's a reputable jeweler," she answered, hating the defensive note that had crept into her voice.

"You're short on cash?"

"I'm fine." There was no way she'd ever tell Lon the truth. She didn't want pity, and she didn't want sympathy from him, either. She'd chosen Clive. End of story. "I didn't realize you were back in the country."

"I have a house in Knightsbridge."

"You live here in London?"

"Part of the year."

"I had no idea."

Lon heard the pang in her voice, and he felt a shaft of hot emotion. He'd known from the start that her marriage had been rocky, maybe even downright unhappy, but she'd never said a word against Clive. "I travel back and forth between South America quite a bit. Depends on business."

He hadn't seen her in years and yet she was still beautiful. More beautiful. If anything, grief had etched her features finer, darkening her eyebrows, softening her mouth, creating deeper hollows beneath her cheekbones. Few women could achieve with plastic surgery what nature had given Sophie so freely.

The jeweler returned with a check which Sophie silently pocketed. Transaction completed, she murmured her thanks and Lon escorted Sophie outside. "What about your business?" she protested.

"The stone's not ready. I'll come back later."

It was cold outside. The late afternoon temperatures dipped low. Sophie took a quick breath, trying to clear her head. *Lon here.* Impossible. Incredible. She'd never once bumped into him in all the years since they'd left Colombia.

She drew her coat closer as throngs of pedestrians pushed past them, and her gaze took in Harrod's festive windows across the street. The ornate building's majestic turrets were illuminated with countless white lights and windows were decked with wreaths.

"It's almost Christmas," Lon said, breaking the uneasy silence between them.

Which meant it'd been almost two years without Clive. Sophie bit her lower lip, fighting tears and the confusing emotions threatening to overwhelm her.

God, she'd missed Lon. He'd been her friend for years and then he'd just disappeared from her life. She struggled to think when she'd last seen him but she couldn't even figure out how long it'd been.

"You still look like a savage," she said huskily.

"And you don't like savages."

"I liked you."

"Past tense?"

Sophie's eyes stung all over again and the wind tugged at her coat, nipping at her skin. What lies they'd told themselves to make her decision all right.

"I have to go home," she said, voice thickening. "The Countess is waiting."

The first raindrop fell from the heavy dark clouds. "I'll take you."

"It's too far. An hour and a half—"

"I'll take you," he repeated, and he practically tucked her beneath his arm, her head against his shoulder, her body pressed to his side.

He was still hard, solid, imposing and she shivered all through her feeling as if she'd been washed overboard and was close to drowning.

He'd only been back in her life twenty minutes and already nothing was the same. But that's how Lon had always been. Huge. Imposing.

In his car, Sophie felt the strangest emotion—crazy emotion—longing, regret, desperation. She thought she'd do just about anything to go back in time and find the teenagers they'd all once been.

"I've missed you, Sophie," he said quietly.

Her heart lurched. *You're far too lonely,* she chided herself even as her heart lurched again. It was a painful jump, much like the painful jumps she'd felt as a teenager when she knew he wanted her and she didn't know what to think, or what to feel.

Hot tears started to her eyes and she blinked. It was embarrassing, being so emotional. She hadn't felt this way in ages. Ever since Clive died she'd been very controlled, very contained, but here she was about to leap out of her skin.

She wanted to blame her nerves on fatigue, stress, holiday jitters, but it was Lon. He'd always done this to her. Tied her up in knots. Made her feel so many things.

He was still magnetic. Compelling. His unusual coloring—very black hair and very light blue eyes—drew attention. He certainly wasn't your typical Englishman, and maybe that's what fascinated the women. He looked foreign. *Dangerous.*

But then, he *was* dangerous.

"What are you looking at?" he asked, shifting and accelerating.

"You." She tried to disguise the intensity of her feelings, but wasn't succeeding. She shouldn't be here alone with him. She couldn't let herself get close to him. They weren't teenagers anymore, and she knew Lon didn't play games. No, Lon played for keeps.

And she didn't do keeps. At least, not with Alonso. He was still too unpredictable, still too intimidating.

Her gaze traveled his broad forehead, the wide jaw, the strong nose before settling on the thin scar running along the edge of Lon's right cheekbone. The scar hadn't been there five years ago. "How did you get that scar?"

"Nicked myself shaving." He leaned back in his deep leather seat. It was a deep scar, an ugly scar. It wasn't a shaving mishap.

"Must have been a big razor."

The corner of his mouth twisted. "Huge."

She couldn't look away from the scar. It should have ruined his hard face. Instead it added strength. Character. With the creases at his eyes and the scar high on his cheek, he looked like a man that knew his way around the world. Like a man who'd come to terms with life. "Did it hurt?"

"Losing you hurt more."

She sucked in a breath and glanced down at her bare hands. Her left hand felt so empty without her heavy ring.

"So you've never married?" she asked, swiftly changing subjects, trying to find safer ground. Clive had told her once that Lon maintained homes and offices in Bogota and Buenos Aires but it seemed like a universe away from her life in England.

"No."

"Engaged?"

"No."

"Live-in girlfriend?"

"You're quite curious, *muñeca*. Are you interested in applying for the job?"

His slow, mocking smile set her heart racing and her limbs felt like lead. Oh, he was still dangerous. He still turned her inside out, made her feel shaky and jittery. "Sorry. Not interested." She should have never gotten into his car, should never have agreed to this. "Living-in is less exciting than fairy tales would lead us to believe."

"The disillusioned princess."

"Hardly a princess."

"No, just an impoverished lady forced to sell her house, her car, and now her wedding ring."

Sophie squeezed her eyes shut. He could hurt her in ways no one else could. "They're just things," she whispered.

"And what are things when you're surrounded by warmth and tenderness and love?"

She almost hated him right now. He was so cold, so cynical. He had to know she was living alone with the Countess, Clive's mother. He knew the Countess, too. He knew she wasn't warm, and he had to know Sophie was virtually trapped at Melrose Court with no personal space, or freedom, anymore.

But she didn't say that, didn't say a word. If he wanted to be cruel, fine, let him. He'd be gone soon. He'd drop her at Melrose Court and drive off into the night and she wouldn't have to deal with him anymore.

"I would have paid you twice as much for your ring, Sophie." Lon's voice broke the silence. "Why didn't you come to me?"

"I don't need your charity."

"It's not charity. The emerald alone was worth twenty thousand pounds. The setting was another ten to fifteen."

She shrugged. Don't think about it, she told herself. You didn't know, and even if you did, you wouldn't have been able to get more. "I'm happy with what he paid me."

"As long as you're happy," he answered, running a hand across his brow, rubbing tiredly.

His hair was long, longer than he'd ever worn it ten years earlier, and the back nearly touched his shoulders. He was too big for the black Porsche. His shoulders filled the car. His hands on the steering wheel were large, his skin burnished from hours in the sun.

But he wasn't just big. He was strong. Immensely powerful. She knew Lon had worked in the mines personally, years before he'd ever bought his share. He hadn't been afraid of the explosives, the tight quarters, the perils of collapsing tunnels and elevator shafts.

What an odd pair they were. Lon, afraid of nothing, and Sophie, afraid of everything.

"How long did the honeymoon last, Sophie?"

She startled, shocked by his nerve. "That's none of your business."

His smile was cool. "I want to know. Tell me. How long did it take before you knew you'd made a mistake?"

Her mouth went dry. She struggled to swallow. "Take that back!"

"Not a chance."

"You have no right—"

"I *loved* you." Lon's voice dropped, his jaw tightening with anger. "Clive never loved you. He just didn't want me to have you."

"No."

"Yes. And you, silly girl, were so damn afraid of your feelings, you ran straight into his arms."

Her head swam, Lon's words nearly making her ill. She reached for the door handle as if she could escape.

But there was no escape. Lon had found her. Lon still wanted her. And deep inside she knew this time Lon would never let her go.

"Do you know what it was like, realizing I'd lost you forever?" He ground his teeth together as he stared straight out the windshield, night falling all around them. But the strain showed in his face, reflected by the dashboard lights, and the greenish dashboard light heightened the paleness of his scar. "I knew you'd never have an affair, either. Good sweet Sophie Johnson would be true to her husband. And you were, weren't you?"

His leather coat had fallen open and his black cashmere sweater was v-necked, a fairly deep v-neck that showed tanned skin and hard muscles. Lon's chest was wide, deep, the thick muscles wrapping his rib cage in sinewy bands.

She blinked back stinging tears. "Of course I was loyal."

"Of course." He smiled but there was no warmth, no mercy in his eyes. "You're loyal to everyone—but me."

Blood rushed to her cheeks and she felt hot and prickly all over. "We were young, Lon. I was young."

"Not that young."

"And it was a long time ago."

"Not long enough for me to forget."

"Lon."

"Don't think it's over, Sophie." His deep voice held her, trancelike, and she found herself looking up at him. His eyes should have been black, but they were the lightest, clearest blue. "It's not even close to being over. You're not even twenty-eight. I'm thirty-two. We've got all the time in the world."

By the time they arrived at Melrose Court, Sophie felt dizzy, her stomach churning so hard she was certain she'd soon be ill. Lon shot her a hard look after parking. "Did you eat anything today?"

"I'm fine." But stepping from the car she was anything but fine. Her legs nearly buckled under her and tears of rage filled her eyes.

Ignoring her protest, Lon swept her up the stairs. "She's feeling a little faint," he informed a startled Countess Wilkins, his arm still wrapped around Sophie's waist. "Could you get a glass of water?"

The Countess disappeared and Lon stared down in her face. "You're looking a little pale, Sophie."

Only Lon would be so ruthless. Only Lon would want to punish her. Yes, she'd liked him all those years ago. And maybe yes, she'd loved him, but he wanted more than her love. He'd wanted everything. All of her. He was like a vortex and he scared the hell out of her.

"I'm not ready to date again," she whispered, conscious that Louisa would return any moment.

"No?"

"No."

"So it's not true about you and…what's his name? Rich, good-looking man. Dark hair, rather like mine, dark eyes—"

"Federico," she interrupted with a soft strangled sound.

"Federico," Lon said slowly, thoughtfully drawing the name out. "Sounds foreign."

Sophie shivered, and her dark blue gaze, dropped. "Aren't we all?"

Any other time Alonso would have smiled. It was true. Just as Lon and Sophie had met as teenagers in Latin America, most people in their sphere had lived all over the world. Diplomats, engineers, miners, bankers, foreign investors. But Lon couldn't smile, not when they were discussing Federico Alvare.

Miguel Valdez was one of Latin America's biggest druglords and Federico Alvare served as his right-hand man. A former MI6 agent, Lon knew Federico personally, and Federico would drag Sophie to hell if he could.

"It's all right if you have a new boyfriend," he continued conversationally, trying to ignore the fire burning through his middle. Sophie and another man? Possibly. Maybe. Barely. Sophie and Federico Alvare? Never. And it was this rumor that had brought him back to England. His contacts said Lady Wilkins was in trouble, that she was associating with one of the world's most dangerous criminals. He hadn't believed it until now. "There's no reason you shouldn't be dating. It's been two years."

"I've no interest in dating again, and he's not a boyfriend. He's just a…friend." Sophie couldn't even meet his gaze, her eyes fixed on a point on the floor. "Federico used to work with Clive."

She was either painfully innocent or damn brazen.

Right now Lon couldn't figure out which. "I had no idea."

Sophie's lower lip quivered and she pressed her lips together, pressing down. Her small pale face suddenly looked tight and a damp tendril slipped from the twist of dark hair pinned up at the back. "No, you wouldn't know. After Clive and I married, you wouldn't have anything to do with us."

He watched, fascinated, as the long tendril clung to the side of her neck. Lucky tendril. Lucky neck. Now he had to protect that pretty neck before something tragic happened. "It was a two way street, Sophie."

"Clive tried," she gritted, her blue eyes fierce. She was wearing a cream sweater dress and the top two buttons had popped open giving him a glimpse of an ivory bra strap.

"Not very hard."

"You never returned his calls. You've no idea how much it hurt him, how much it hurt both of us."

Lon was perfectly happy letting Sophie talk. He was too interested in the open buttons of her sweater dress, the hint of creamy breast, the long pale column of her throat, her very sweet mouth...

Sophie's lips, even without lipstick, were full and pink and right now all he wanted to do was drink the angry words from her mouth, draw the air from her lungs, fold her into him.

His body hardened just looking at her. He physically craved Sophie. His mind wanted her mind. His skin wanted her skin. His body wanted to be lost in hers.

"You could have called me," he said even as the Countess returned with the glass of water.

"I can't tell you how pleased I am to see you," Louisa Wilkins said, giving Alonso a brief embrace. "It's been years. Two years. Since Clive's funeral, I believe."

Lon heard Sophie's swift inhale and felt her stiffen. "I think you're right," he answered, anxious to move on to less sensitive topics. "But you look wonderful, Louisa, not a day older."

The Countess practically beamed. She'd missed male company, too. "Thank you, Alonso. Very kind of you to say. And you are staying for dinner, aren't you?"

Sophie's blue eyes looked panicked. "I think he's busy, Louisa."

"Not that busy," Lon corrected. "I'd love to stay."

The Countess folded her hands over her stomach. "I'll have Cook add another place to the table." She turned to Sophie. "And Sophie, show Alonso the whiskey. If I remember, he likes a good drink before dinner."

In the library Sophie watched Lon pour himself a neat shot. "It seems she's developed a soft spot for you."

Alonso capped the crystal whiskey decanter. "It's the holiday season. She's feeling nostalgic." He sipped from his crystal tumbler. "I imagine Christmas is quite difficult for her."

Sophie said nothing. She just took a seat on the slip-covered sofa and curled her legs beneath her.

"It must be difficult for *you* living alone with the Countess here," he said far more calmly than he felt. On the inside he was growing angry. Irritated. He didn't like losing his temper.

Other officers had kidded him that when pushed, he had an almost superhuman strength, and it was true, he could lift twice his body weight. Easily. Once in training camp he'd clean and jerked 600 kilos and others had just gaped. He'd told them it ran in his family, that his dad was a miner from Scotland, but it was only part of the truth.

His stepfather was Scottish, and a miner. His biological father was an Argentine aristocrat who killed himself by driving a hundred miles an hour into a tree. Drunk, of course.

It was Lon's Argentine blood that got him in trouble.

Sophie shifted miserably. "Louisa's been very good to me."

Talk about laughable. The Countess had always treated Sophie like a second-class citizen. But maybe he was being too harsh. Maybe things had changed. "She looks well," he said. "But how is she really doing?"

"She's in remarkably good health, and of course, this time of year, she's very focused on the ball."

"Oh yes. The annual Wilkins Christmas Gala. I received my invitation last week."

Sophie couldn't hide her surprise. "You got an invitation?"

"I get one every year." Lon answered with satisfaction. He knew, just as she did, that the Countess had never particularly liked him. "I've just never been in the country before."

"You're attending, then?"

He heard the wobble in her voice. She didn't want him to attend. Interesting. "Should I?"

"No." She flushed, and added quickly, "It's just not your kind of party. Hundreds of people. Not enough food. I don't think you'd even know anyone attending."

"But it'd be worth it if I could see you."

Sophie started to rise and then sat down again. She pressed her hands tightly to the sofa cushion. "Nothing's going to happen between us, Lon. I'm not over Clive. I'm not ready for anything new—"

"I'm not new."

How true, she thought, feeling her heart mash in her chest. He wasn't new. He'd been part of her world for nearly fifteen years but fifteen years ago he hadn't been right for her. Ten years ago he hadn't been right. And even today, he wasn't what she needed. "Please do not make this ugly, Lon. Do not force me to be rude."

"You? Rude?" He laughed without humor. "You couldn't be rude if you tried. You've made diplomacy an art form. You turned tact into a virtue. You can rest now, Sophie. You're the martyr you always wanted to be."

Her head swam. She sank her fingers into the old down-filled cushion. He was so good at wounding her. So good at finding the jugular. "And you, Lon, do you enjoy being deliberately unkind?"

He watched her delicate features tighten, her mouth pinching, her voice dropping so her words were barely audible.

She looked so fragile sitting on the edge of the over-stuffed sofa, so unlike all the cool, casual women he'd learned to fill his life with.

Sophie wasn't cool and casual. She was rare, and beautiful, almost otherworldly, and he'd once wanted her so badly that losing her had been a death.

Yes. He had been deliberately unkind. He'd meant to hurt her. Deep down he still wanted her to suffer for choosing Clive instead of him.

He'd lost his heart the day he walked Sophie down the aisle, literally handing her over to Clive.

He'd never said it aloud, couldn't even dwell on the memory, but he'd hated her for asking him to walk her down the aisle. He'd hated filling in for her father who was too ill to participate in the wedding. He'd hated that she'd even try to turn him into family...a surrogate brother or parent.

He didn't want to be her father.

He wanted to be her lover.

"No," he answered grimly. "I don't enjoy being unkind. I just am."

CHAPTER TWO

LON shook his head regretfully. "It seems as if I've enormous control, Lady Wilkins, except when it comes to you."

"And you wonder why Clive felt uncomfortable around you after we married?" She choked, rising from the sofa.

No, he didn't wonder why Clive felt uncomfortable around him—he *knew*. But he couldn't tell Sophie that, couldn't tell her anything of Clive's secret past. Clive had never told her who he was—or what he'd become—and although Lon knew, he'd vowed years ago to protect Sophie from the truth. Because the truth would crush her, just as it'd crushed him.

Clive had been one of them, one with them. He wasn't supposed to turn into a stranger...

Emotions hot, memories tangled, Lon marched toward her. "If Clive and I grew apart, it wasn't due to my civility—"

"Or lack of," she interrupted fiercely, taking a step backward. She didn't have room to move. The sofa was behind her. Lon in front of her. "You were everything to Clive. He adored you. You know he did. You were his very best friend in the world. So why would he pull away from you? What happened?"

"We grew up."

"It can't be that simple. You had been best friends for years. You did everything together. Same boarding school. Same university. Same friends. He even applied to the Royal Air Force when you did."

Lon's blue gaze glowed down at her. "Maybe it was

21

too much togetherness. Maybe Clive would have done better making new friends, surrounding himself with people. Because I don't think I was that good for Clive. I don't think I made him feel good about himself.''

They were heading into uncharted territory here. She knew Lon had been angry with Clive for a long time now and she needed to understand, just as she needed to understand what happened to Clive in Brazil. ''*Why* weren't you good for Clive? How did you stop making him feel good about himself?''

He hesitated, as if unwilling to go where she wanted to go. ''We...changed,'' he said finally. ''We grew apart.''

She couldn't let this go. This was part of the mystery surrounding Clive, part of the mystery surrounding the demise of her marriage. ''Clive didn't change. You must have changed—''

''Clive changed, too. Clive could be very complicated.''

Clive, complicated? Sophie didn't believe it for an instant. Clive was the least complicated person she'd ever known. ''You're not making sense. I know you, Lon, I know you can be direct, but you're speaking 'round the subject right now. You're not telling me anything that I don't already know.''

''And what good would it do you, to tell you why Clive and I had a falling out? How will it help?'' He reached for her, adjusted the cream knit collar on her sweater dress. ''We were friends, the three of us, and I don't want to hurt him. I don't want to hurt you.'' His fingers brushed the side of her neck.

She felt an arrow of pleasure pierce her neck and then shoot fire through her middle. Sophie balled her hands, trying to deny the coil of desire and pleasure.

Life wasn't about desire, or pleasure. Life required a cool, calm head. Life required practicality.

And Lon was the least practical man she knew.

Sophie held her breath, trying to hang on to the anger, trying to keep from letting her feelings intensify. Remember who he really is, she silently reminded herself. Lon's a traveling man. She was right to pick Clive. Lon never sticks around. He's the ultimate bachelor—no ties, no roots, no children, no home.

During their boarding school days Lon was one of the students that never went home. Not on weekends. And not even for most school holidays.

She'd thought it was his mother's choice for years, and it wasn't until they'd matriculated that she learned it'd been Lon's choice. Lon couldn't bear to live with his mother and new stepfather.

"Do you ever see your mom anymore?" she asked, trying to ignore his hand that remained on her collar, his touch light, deft, even as she tried to ignore the old ache that had returned to her chest. He made her feel so much...

Too much.

The intensity scared her. Still.

"When I can," he answered, his gaze holding hers, his blue eyes shadowed with secrets he never shared. His blue eyes had been shadowy like that as a teenager at Langley, and yet as he, Clive and Sophie left school, the shadows had cleared. But the darkness was back again. The hardness, too. "Mother and Boyd have returned to Scotland. They live just outside Edinburgh. I've promised Mother I'd join them for Christmas. I'll probably return to London on Boxing Day."

And on Boxing Day she'd be boarding a plane for Brazil. "Are they well?"

"Yes. They're enjoying Boyd's retirement. And you," Lon said, tugging gently on her collar. "How are you? Are you happy?"

His deep, rough voice went all the way through her and she shivered inside, shivered with a longing that she couldn't control. Lon still overpowered her in every way possible.

"Happy?" she whispered, knowing that even if she couldn't love him the way he'd wanted her to, she couldn't hate him, either. "My husband's dead. I've lost my home. I depend on my mother-in-law's generosity." Her eyes met his. "What do you think?"

His thumb brushed her chin. "I think you need me."

"You're still unbelievably arrogant."

"And you're still deep in denial."

The library doors opened abruptly. The Countess entered, extending a hand to Alonso. "Dinner, my dear, is served."

During dinner, Countess Louisa was in fine form, regaling Lon with story after story.

The Countess was one of the worst storytellers alive, but Lon, bless him, listened attentively as Louisa described the Somerset Ladies Horticultural Association's autumn plans in stunningly dry detail.

Sophie wondered how Lon could possibly keep a straight face. Ten years ago Lon would have never listened to Louisa's dull stories.

But then, ten years ago Louisa wouldn't have talked to Lon.

They'd all changed so much in the past ten years. No, make that the past five years. Losing Clive had changed everything for them.

Lon looked up and his gaze met hers. She could have sworn he knew what she was thinking, and he looked at her with so much warmth, and hunger, Sophie felt breathless with curiosity.

Would he ever kiss her again?

Would he—could he—make her feel what she'd once felt when she was eighteen and still so excited about life?

The Countess rattled her cup as she returned it to the saucer. "Have you had enough dessert, my dear?" Her question was addressed to Lon.

"Yes, Louisa. Thank you."

"Then you'll join me in the library," Louisa stated, pushing away from the table even as Sophie rose and began stacking the dishes.

"Why don't I stay and help Sophie clear the table?"

The Countess waved her hand. "Nonsense. Sophie's fine." Louisa sailed forward and took Lon's arm as if he were the last man alive. "Aren't you, Sophie?"

"I'm fine," she agreed, not because she couldn't use the help in the kitchen, but because she needed a few minutes alone to pull herself together.

Seeing Lon—talking to Lon—discussing the past, had thrown her into a tailspin. She was supposed to be concentrating on her trip to Brazil. Instead at the moment all she could think about was Lon, and the way it'd once been between them.

But wasn't this how she'd always felt around him? Dazed. Nervous? Hopelessly excited?

"I'm fine," she repeated more firmly, this time for her sake, not his. She wasn't a teenager anymore. She'd become a woman. A wife. And now a widow. If she could handle all those life changes, she could certainly handle an evening with Alonso. "I'll join you as soon as I'm done."

Sophie was elbow deep in soap bubbles when a long arm covered in fine black cashmere stretched past her, and picked up a dish towel.

"What are you doing?" she asked, turning to get a glimpse of Lon.

He'd pushed up his sleeves and was applying the dish

towel to one of the rinsed dinner plates. "Helping you finish."

"The Countess won't like it."

"The Countess doesn't know. She thinks I'm in the lavatory." He grinned, and his smile was so boyish, so much like the Lon she remembered from their summer holiday, that Sophie's heart tightened, too full of memories and pain.

"You haven't really changed," she said, shooting him a dark glance.

"No. And you wouldn't want me to. Now hand me the next plate." Again his arm reached past her and she felt a tingle of pleasure as he brushed her hip with his own.

"How long have you been staying with the Countess?" he asked.

Her whole body felt far too sensitive. "A little over a year now," she answered hoarsely. "Ever since Humphrey House was closed." Humphrey House had been the house Clive took her to as a bride. "I couldn't manage the maintenance and repairs anymore."

"What's it like living with her?"

"Interesting."

"But you two must be getting along to survive a year?"

"I haven't had much choice though, have I?" And then she shrugged. "But things are fine. I'm fine. I'm lucky she's opened her home to me."

"But?"

"There's no but. England's not South America. It'll never be South America."

He reached for the last plate. "So you think about Colombia?"

She smiled. "All the time." Her voice dropped, and she stared into the sudsy water for a long moment. "They were the best years of my life."

That was telling, Lon thought. She'd been an outcast

at Elmshurst. There were two other Americans at the elite girls boarding school, but they were both very wealthy, and very connected. Sophie was neither. "What do you remember when you think about Columbia?"

"Buenaventura."

The school holiday at the Wilkins beach house. Clive had managed to convince his father to invite both Lon and Sophie that summer.

Dishes done, Sophie pulled the plug on the sink. "It was an amazing holiday."

Lon's chest felt tight. She sounded so wistful. So alone. Did she even know how lonely she was? "Come home with me for Christmas," he said impulsively, thinking she'd be happier—and safer—with him. He needed to keep her away from Federico, needed to make sure she wouldn't do anything foolish over the holidays. "My mother would be pleased to have you join us. It'd be a quiet Christmas—"

"I can't leave Louisa here alone," Sophie interrupted.

"She can come."

"She won't."

"Then that's her choice, but you shouldn't let her decisions influence you."

She hesitated. Her expression grew pensive. "How is your mother and Boyd these days?"

"Learning to peacefully coexist."

"It's been nearly twenty years."

"It took her a long time to stop comparing Boyd to my father."

"Poor Boyd!"

"He knew my mother was marrying him on the rebound. He knew theirs wasn't a love match." Lon was smiling as he leaned against the counter but Sophie felt a quiet menace in him. "You never did like my mother, did you?"

Sophie wished this topic had never come up. She didn't know how to extract herself gracefully. She and Lon had known each other too long to lie. "I've never understood her."

His eyes narrowed fractionally. "What's there to understand?"

"You were the one that told me she'd had an affair with a married man for years."

"The affair was with my father."

Sophie swallowed. She heard the steely note in Lon's voice and knew she'd touched a nerve. "I just don't understand how she could put you through that...you were just a little boy..."

"He loved her. She loved him—"

"He was married! What about his wife's feelings? What about his other children's feelings? How could your mother not see how hurtful it was for you to only see your father now and then? To never have a father there at Christmas, or on your birthday?"

Lon's jaw hardened. "He sent cards, and gifts."

"Cards. Gifts." Anger burned in her. "And *gifts* were supposed to make up for a selfish, absentee father, a depressed mother, and a broken home?"

"It was her heart, her life—"

"No! It was *your* heart. *Your* life. Her choices impacted you, too!" She spat the words at him, and suddenly Sophie saw her own home, and her own family. She wasn't just upset for Lon. She was upset for herself. She'd lived through such loneliness as a little girl. She knew what it was like to have an absentee parent. Her mother had walked out on them when she was small and her father had spent the rest of his life struggling to make things okay.

Okay.

As if anything would ever really be *okay* again.

But Lon didn't know that Sophie's hostility was directed at her own mother as well as his and he'd taken another step away from her. "I had no idea how much you disliked my mother."

"I don't—"

"She doesn't need you judging her. She doesn't need anyone judging her. She's allowed to make her own mistakes, just as you've made yours."

"What mistakes?"

"Still playing ostrich, aren't you?" he retorted, dropping the damp dish towel on the counter and walking out.

As Sophie watched Lon walk away her heart felt like it was being ripped in two.

They'd once been so close. He'd been the most important person in her life. How had it come to this? Why had it come to this?

Clive.

Sophie reached up, pressed the palm of her hand to her temple. Her head felt as if it were so heavy, so unbelievably tired. She'd been trying to keep so much secret, and hidden inside, but all the details, all the travel and party problems, were overwhelming her.

There was only so much one could remember...only so much one could do...

If she could just get Louisa's gala behind her.

If she could just keep Lon from meeting Federico.

If she could just get on the plane and head for Brazil...

Just another couple days, she reminded herself. *Hang in there. Be patient. You'll be in Sao Paulo before you know it.*

Sophie drew a deep breath, and pulled her shoulders back. Time to go face Louisa and Alonso.

Not that she wanted to.

"Ah, there she is," Louisa said, turning and indicating Sophie's presence, as Sophie entered the semidark ballroom. "We were just wondering if you'd washed yourself down the sink."

"Oh, no, nothing as exciting as that." Sophie answered, glancing at Lon. But he wouldn't make eye contact.

Instead he glanced at his watch. "It's time I headed back to London." He leaned toward Louisa, kissed her on the cheek. "Thank you for a lovely evening."

"My pleasure." Louisa laid a hand on his arm. "And I trust we'll have your company at the ball on Saturday?"

"Unfortunately I've had plans for quite some time."

"What a shame. Sophie's invited some of her other friends. I'm sure you'd enjoy them."

"I'm sure I would, too." His smile was tight. It didn't reach his eyes. "Happy Christmas, Louisa."

Sophie walked with Lon through the rest of the ballroom. Though the grand room was empty now, it'd be transformed in three days time with a twelve foot tall tree in the corner, garland at the doors, and fragrant boughs at the windows.

"It's going to be quite a party," Lon said, stopping to look behind them.

Sophie knew that just decorating the enormous tree would take her and two staff members all day. "It always is."

He looked down at her, no smile anywhere in his hard blue gaze. "Will I know any of your guests?"

Blood surged to her cheeks. "I don't think so."

He studied her expression for a long, tense moment. "You make me nervous, Sophie."

She forced a laugh. "You, nervous? Come on Lon. You're Superman. Only thing you're afraid of is kryptonite!" And she moved on, toward the front door, feeling as if she were walking a tightrope.

She couldn't manage her feelings around Lon.

She couldn't manage Lon.

And she couldn't forget the past. Her life felt nearly impossible now. Ever since Clive died she'd struggled along, confused. Disoriented. It was grief, some said, but for Sophie it was more.

She reached the entry and faced the second floor landing where Wilkins family portraits covered the pale green walls.

Something terrible had happened to her husband in Sao Paulo and Sophie needed to know. She had to understand or she'd never get any peace, never mind closure.

"I miss him, Lon," she said as she heard Lon's footsteps sound behind her. "I miss Clive. I miss his optimism and most of all, I miss the way he laughed. Sometimes I can't believe it's only been two years since he died. It feels like ten."

"He'd hate what he's done to you, Sophie," Lon said tightly. "He'd hate that he left you like this—"

"He made a mistake."

"He made dozens."

"Don't." She turned to face Lon, pain washing over her in waves. "Don't criticize him. Not now, not with him gone. I can't bear it." And she couldn't. As it was, Clive's death weighed on her, torturing her.

It was her fault, she thought. Karma. Payback. *Revenge.*

Lon's hand rested on the ornate doorknob. "He'd hate you trapped here at Melrose Court, he'd hate that you've been left with so little and have to struggle alone like this—"

"It's not his fault," she interrupted hoarsely, unable to let him continue, unable to see herself the way Lon saw her.

Lon didn't know her. Lon didn't know the truth.

She wasn't a good virtuous woman. She wasn't the loyal loving wife she'd pretended to be.

Karma, talk about karma. She'd filed for divorce only one day before the telegram arrived announcing Clive's death.

One day before he died. Could punishment be any swifter? It was as if the gods had said, you want to be free, lady? Wish granted—be free! Want to go it alone? Do it!

She turned away again, moving up the stairwell once more to find Clive's portrait on the landing. Clive's portrait hung next to his father's, and staring at Clive's handsome features, with his shock of blond hair, she felt like a traitor.

Her eyes burned, her nose burned, her throat burned, but the burning was nothing like the fire raging inside her heart.

Clive had tried his best and yet his love hadn't been enough. She'd still wanted more.

Still needed more.

Her disloyalty had killed Clive, and as much as she cared for Alonso, as much as she craved his warmth and his strength, as much as she needed him emotionally *and* physically, she couldn't have him. It'd be like rewarding herself for her sins.

"I know you miss him," Lon said quietly, "but you have to move forward, not back."

Her throat ached with all the tears she wouldn't let fall. She'd never forget the day she received the telegram from the British consulate in Brazil. *Lady Wilkins, we regret to inform you…*

Sophie looked up, shook her head. Clive had only been twenty-nine. *Twenty-nine.* Far too young to die. "How can I move forward if I don't understand the past? I don't understand how Clive died, or why he died…"

"He was in the wrong place at the wrong time."

She shuddered, imagining Clive's final minutes.

Apparently Clive had been shot at close range. "But why? Why would he be there? What would take him to that neighborhood at that time of night?"

"I don't think we'll ever know," Lon answered, opening the door and stepping outside. He froze on the doorstep.

Beyond Alonso's big shoulders Sophie saw huge white flakes slowly fall. The landscape shone white, the sky a curtain of swirling snow.

"It's *snowing*." She joined Lon at the door, quarrel momentarily forgotten. "It's beautiful."

"I haven't seen snow in years."

Sophie followed him outside, and the wind gusted, blowing white flakes in through the door. She reached up to catch the delicate flakes landing on her cheeks and in her hair. The night was so quiet, so perfectly still, and it made her heart ache.

For her, for Clive, for Lon. For all of them.

"How did we come to this, Lon?" she whispered, crossing her arms over her chest and watching the snow flurries fall.

"We grew up."

Her eyes felt hot and gritty. "We were supposed to always be friends. We were the Three Musketeers."

The corner of Lon's mouth lifted. *"Tres amigos."*

The three buddies…the three friends. Clive, Lon, and Sophie. Her eyes felt raw. Her throat was sore. She'd been holding back the emotion all night, trying to contain the staggering hurt and need. "How do we fix this? How do we make it right?"

He glanced down at her, his expression curiously gentle. "We focus on the future. We make the rest of our lives as meaningful as possible."

"But that would mean leaving Clive behind."

Lon didn't answer and hot tears filled her eyes. She

wished she could move toward Lon, move into his arms and feel his warmth, his strength. "I don't want to fight with you anymore." Her voice sounded raspy. "I want to be friends with you again, and I'm sorry for what I said to you earlier. I'm sorry that I said what I did about your mom. I don't dislike her. I know she's had a hard life."

He shrugged uncomfortably. "It's been an unconventional life. But it's what she wanted, and she's learned to be happy."

Sophie looked out at the horizon where the powdery snow reflected the moonlight, and the gently rolling landscape glittered and shone as far as the eye could see.

Lon brushed a snowflake from her temple. "You can learn to be happy, too, Sophie. It's just a matter of choosing happiness."

His touch made her feel hot, tingly. She balled her fingers. How could Lon still make her feel this way? The snow was dusting his black leather coat, clinging to his hair, his lashes. "You make it sound simple."

"It is." Lon drew his car keys from his pocket. "So what are you wearing to the gala?" He asked, smiling, trying to lighten the mood.

She made a face. "My standard black."

"Clive hated you in black."

She grimaced again. Clive did hate her in black. Everything he ever gave her was saturated in color. Yellows, reds, blues, greens. "Black's practical."

"At least you didn't say slimming." Lon's smile disappeared and he stared at her for a long, pensive moment. His inspection was intense, intimate and she grew warm all over. He looked at her with undisguised desire.

"I lost you once," he said quietly. "Don't think I'm going to lose you again."

CHAPTER THREE

SATURDAY evening Sophie dressed for the party, and even though she was going to wear her black gown—the one she'd worn the past two years—she put on her best lingerie underneath. Maybe she didn't have jewels but that didn't mean she couldn't put her best foot forward.

The black lace garter belt fit snugly around her waist and she carefully rolled the delicate silk hose up each ankle, over her calves, over the knees to the top of her thigh where she attached the tiny black garter strap.

She snapped the hooks on her black lace strapless bra and stepped into her gown.

Sophie stared at her reflection in the mirror.

Black, black, black.

She didn't want to feel this way; hated feeling this way. It was nearly Christmas for heaven's sake! She'd made a mistake, but couldn't she ever be happy again? Would it be so awful if she just looked pretty one more time?

If she just felt festive once?

Forgive me, Clive, she whispered, and peeled the black dress off her shoulders and down past her hips.

Standing in her closet she stared at the few gowns she had left, including the one dress she wanted to wear, the one dress she'd never worn. It'd been bought for her honeymoon with Clive and yet the resort they went to turned out to be quite casual.

There was a knock at the bedroom door. "Sophie, it's half six and the guests will be arriving soon."

"I'm already ready, Louisa," Sophie answered, reaching for the red gown.

The bedroom door opened and Louisa appeared in full party regalia: long gray satin dress, diamond and pearl necklace, diamond and pearl brooch, diamond and pearl earrings, even a little diamond and pearl tiara tucked into her puffy silver hair. "You're not even close to being ready!"

Sophie pulled the shimmering strapless red shantung silk dress from the closet. "All I have to do is zip it."

"You're going to wear that?" Louisa eyed the red dress with suspicion. "What about your black gown?"

"I've worn that two years in a row—"

"And it looks *splendid* on you."

"Clive bought me this dress," she said, stepping into the slim long skirt with the small train. But she wasn't thinking of Clive. She was thinking of Lon—even though he wasn't coming tonight. "I'll be downstairs in just a moment."

Downstairs Sophie did a last minute inspection. The ballroom glittered. The six magnificent chandeliers with the five thousand crystals shone on the polished stone floor and the enormous Christmas tree in the corner. The small orchestra was playing a Strauss waltz and even though no guests had arrived yet, the scene felt magical—like marzipan confections painted and dusted in sparkling sugar.

She spent the first hour of the party greeting guests at the front door, collecting coats, accepting hostess gifts, and generally making visitors feel welcome.

At least, that had been her objective until Lon showed up with a bouquet of white lilies he placed in Sophie's arms.

"What are you doing here?" she choked, stunned to see Alonso slide a long black wool overcoat from his shoulders, revealing a gorgeous tuxedo beneath.

"The Countess can't hire staff for this job?" he replied, leaning down and greeting her with a kiss.

She turned her head so his lips brushed her cheek. "Don't start," she whispered into his ear.

He held her a moment longer than necessary and then kissed the side of her neck, just below her ear. "I haven't even begun."

His voice hummed in her, as did the suggestive promise. She struggled to catch her breath, overwhelmed by the rush of sensation, the zing of adrenaline.

He'd barely kissed her. How could such a light touch be so electric? How could such a fleeting brush against her neck make her feel so hot and tense?

"I had a change of plans," he said, stepping away, adjusting the cuffs on his dress shirt. "Fortunate, isn't it?"

No. What she felt for Lon was crazy and intense and she couldn't stand the tangled emotions he stirred within her. "I'll give the flowers to Louisa," she answered, grateful for the appearance of new guests arriving. Someone had to save her from Alonso. It'd once been Clive's job, but he couldn't do that anymore.

"They're for you. If I brought Louisa flowers, they'd be yellow mums." He continued to study her, his narrowed gaze taking in every detail of her snug red gown, the matching red shoes peeping from beneath the hem, the twist and loop of her long hair—fastened low at her nape so coiled tendrils fell between her bare shoulder blades.

"Have any of your friends arrived?" he asked, finishing his inspection, his gaze resting on her bare throat and ears.

"Uh—no." She tensed. "You're the first."

"I'm glad it worked out that I could come. I'm really looking forward to meeting all these wonderful friends."

Friends. She fought panic. Her friends were actually just one, and the one happened to be Federico Alvare. And somehow she thought Lon already knew...

"Are these the same friends you're going to Brazil with?" he persisted.

Sophie inhaled sharply. How did he know she was going to Brazil? How *could* he know? She'd told no one. No one, that is, but Federico...

Lon's eyes never left her face. "Why don't we find some water for your flowers, Sophie?"

"I can't. The guests—"

"Oh, yes you can," he interrupted gently, kindly. "The guests are fine. It's you, darling, I'm worried about."

She took a small step backward. She didn't like Lon like this. He was even more frightening. Far too intimidating. "There's no reason to be worried—"

"When were you going to tell me about your holiday plans, Sophie? Or were you just going to sneak away with Federico without telling me?"

It felt as if the floor had dropped out from beneath her. A moment ago she'd felt so hot she wanted to peel off her dress, and now she felt covered in frost. Again her thoughts spun, wondering how could he know such a thing? How did he find out?

Lon saw Sophie swallow, a convulsive little swallow. She was afraid.

She should be. If Sophie landed in Sao Paulo with Federico, Miguel Valdez would skin her alive.

"Maybe we should go to the library," she whispered.

"Good idea."

In the library he closed the paneled doors behind them. "I want to hear everything."

"There's not much to tell."

"The jury's out on that, love."

They stared at each other from across the library. Lon

rather admired Sophie's verve. She was showing more spirit than she'd shown in years. But her confidence was misplaced. She had no idea what she was doing. No idea who she was dealing with. "Does the Countess know?"

"What do you think?" Her hands balled into fists. "And how did you find out, anyway?"

"Is that what you're most worried about?"

She couldn't read his mood. His blue eyes, that strange startling ice blue, were devoid of any emotion. She couldn't read him at all right now. "What should I be worried about?"

"How about draining your bank account? Handing over ten thousand pounds to a complete stranger—because you don't know Federico Alvare, and you did give him the money, didn't you?"

She couldn't answer. She stared at him and curled her fingers into her hands.

"You applied for a Brazilian visa," he continued. "You had Federico buy you an airline ticket."

They were booked on a flight on December 26th. Federico had made the plans. He'd booked the tickets, too. "There's no reason I can't go on holiday. I haven't had a holiday since Clive died."

"Clive died in Brazil."

"So I'm not allowed to visit the country now?"

"Not if you intend to visit the rough neighborhood in Sao Paulo where he died."

She held his gaze. "Is there something I should know about his death? Something you haven't told me? Because you were the one that arranged to have his body sent home."

"I helped with the funeral arrangements. But it's your good friend, Federico, who worked with Clive in Brazil. Have you asked Federico about your husband's death? I'm sure Señor Alvare should have a few…details."

"He does know people in Sao Paulo who might be able to help me. He's secured the services of a private investigator."

Lon smiled thinly. "Federico's hiring you a private investigator?"

She lifted her chin. "Why shouldn't he?"

"Because he's not to be trusted. He's dangerous—"

"And you're not?" she flashed, unable to keep her temper. Alonso could be just as intimidating as Federico…if not more so.

He made a sound of disgust. "You don't even know the meaning of dangerous, *muñeca,* and Alvare is taking total advantage of you if he's charging you ten thousand pounds for your trip."

"Half of it is to cover travel expenses, the other half is for the private investigator."

"It doesn't cost five thousand pounds to get to Brazil, and if you want someone to show you around—"

"This is my trip," she interrupted fiercely. "These are my contacts, *my* plans. I used to live in South America. I'm not totally unfamiliar with the dangers of traveling, and what's ten thousand pounds if it brings me peace? Ten thousand pounds is *nothing* to you. It's chump change in your world."

"In *my* world." He laughed, softly, unkindly, and moved to the beverage cart with the Irish crystal decanters of whiskey and brandy. Lon poured himself a neat shot into a Waterford tumbler. "My, our situations are reversed, aren't they? Amazing the difference just ten years can make."

Strains of music seeped through the closed library doors, as did the high echo of laughter. The guests would be dancing now—Countess Wilkins' parties ran like clockwork. "You've been lucky," she said tautly, drawing her arms closer against her body.

"Luck had nothing to do with it. It was work." He gave his drink a swirl, glancing down briefly at the glints of amber and gold before his gaze settled on her. "Hard work."

Whether it was luck or hard work, he had millions. Millions of pounds in raw minerals. He owned one of Latin America's largest emerald mines. He'd parlayed his earnings into high-tech investments, satellites and computer chips. He could buy and sell small countries in cash. Many people might call themselves high-tech millionaires these days, but few rivaled Alonso's stunning success.

One of Lon's black eyebrows lifted, his blue eyes piercing hers. "Tell me, if I'd been 'filthy rich' five years ago would you have married me instead of Clive?"

Her heart fell, and she struggled to contain her temper, forcing herself to look away from the mockery in his intense gaze to the thin white scar running from the corner of his eye to the edge of his cheekbone. "I did not marry Clive for money."

Lon's eyes crinkled at the corners but he wasn't smiling. "He didn't have any, did he?"

"You were supposed to be his best friend. He adored you, worshiped the ground you walked on—"

"Spare me the histrionics, love. You might have married the man, but I know Clive better than you. He wasn't a Boy Scout. Not even close."

Evil man. God, she hated him right now. "Get out." She walked swiftly to the double doors, her long gleaming red silk gown rustled with each step, and yanked open the library door. "I'll give the Countess your apologies. She'll be disappointed you had to leave so early, but sadly, business called you away."

Lon didn't move from the fireplace. "I have no pressing business."

"I want you to go!"

"Close the door, Sophie. You're drawing a draft."

"I will *not* tolerate you degrading my husband in his own home."

"But this was never his house. It's his mother's house, just as Humphrey House was his father's house. Admit it. Clive never even owned a flat of his own."

Fresh color surged through her cheeks and she felt her composure begin to slip. Nervously she pressed a hand to her stomach, smoothing the expensive fabric, even as she struggled to gain control of the conversation.

This was just Alonso, she sharply reminded herself, a heathen, a misfit, a lost soul without the benefit of a proper upbringing—raised by neither his real father nor his mother—sent off to boarding schools at age four.

Yet only ten years ago he'd been one of her best friends and they'd talked openly about everything—love, life…sex. What the future would be like for them. What they'd once believed the future would be.

Well, the future had arrived and it wasn't even close to the dreams they'd had.

Sophie drew a shallow, painful breath, and she slowly closed the library doors, trying to buy time.

Lon couldn't hurt her, she reminded herself, the spike of pain giving way to a numbing sensation. He couldn't hurt her if she didn't let him. "An apology is in order."

"I'm sorry, Sophie," he answered obediently, loosening the bow tie a bit before unbuttoning the top button of his crisp white dress shirt. He looked sinfully sophisticated. Wicked. *Sexual.* "I'm sorry to quarrel with you."

Her gaze searched his face, noting the fine lines fanning his eyes. He was getting older. Harder. More ruthless. "It's Clive you owe an apology, Clive you've insulted."

"Darling, Clive can't hear me."

Why did Lon have to do this? Why did he have to persist in this blatant unkindness? Yes, he'd had a rough childhood—who hadn't?—but after a while excuses grew old, sympathy cold. One had to grow up. Assume responsibility. "I can't respect a man like you!"

He laughed. "Yet you'll ask me for help whenever things get rough."

Sophie tensed, muscles in her back screaming, head throbbing. Her control felt dangerously threatened. *Just walk away,* she told herself. *Leave him. He'll find his way out.*

But she couldn't ignore Lon, and instead of walking away, she moved toward him, muscles tight and trembling, emotions seething. "Maybe once I asked for your help—"

"Once?" he interrupted. "Sophie, it was more than one time."

She flinched at his scathing tone. "Whenever I've asked for anything, it was for Clive." Two years after their wedding, Clive had been overseas when war broke out in the small Third World country, and the government in power, under siege, closed the small airport, trapping Clive in the middle of the turmoil.

"But you did ask me to help."

So Lon was right again. Pop the champagne. A celebration was in order. Long live King Lon. He never screwed up...well, not after messing up the first twenty years of his life.

"I wasn't going to lose Clive." She lifted her chin, stared Lon down, heart burning, rage consuming her. Clive had managed to call her a day after the airport closed, and while he talked all she could hear was the rat-a-tat-tat of gunfire in the background. He'd called to tell her goodbye, but Sophie had refused to accept defeat, refused to think her marriage would end so ingloriously.

She'd tracked down Alonso, and even though it'd been

years since they'd last spoken, he agreed to do what he could.

Sophie had never asked what that meant. But she'd known that he would rescue Clive. She knew with his courage, his international business, and his many connections, he could do what most people couldn't. And he had. He'd plucked not just Clive—but forty-some other European and Australian nationals—from the middle of the violent coup and brought them home again.

"But that wasn't the only time," Lon said softly. "When have I ever told you no, Sophie?"

Her eyes closed in admission and defeat. Twenty-four months ago Lon stepped in again when Clive died in Brazil.

Lon had taken care of everything from getting Clive's body returned to England to squashing the rumors circulating after Clive's death. Unidentified sources claimed that Lord Clive Wilkins had been involved in something shady in South America, and Lon had nipped that gossip in the bud.

Laughter echoed once more from the ballroom. Sophie turned her head slightly, listening to the sounds of the party. She should be there. She should go. But she didn't move. It was as if Alonso held her captive, an invisible chain tethering her to him.

But she hated the chain. Feared it, even. He would control her, hold her, bind her to him forever if she gave him the chance. And as seductive as it sounded, she couldn't do it, couldn't give in to it.

Sophie looked at him. She might as well have reached out and touched him. Hot, painful sensation shot through her, a ricochet of love and lust. He was still so big. His tuxedo did little to diminish his height or hide his brawny strength. *Gladiator,* Clive had once whispered to her, mocking Alonso's size and strength. *Spartacus,* she added, giggling, feeling safe with Clive, so secure.

The room crackled with tension. Lon could be a savage. She knew the lengths he would go to—knew that when Clive was in danger only Lon would have the heart and guts to get him out. And she felt the wild, savage streak now. Heard it in the implacable edge in his voice. Saw it in the hard glint in his eyes.

He knew what he wanted. He got what he wanted. *Every time.*

This is exactly why she hadn't married Lon. This is exactly why she'd run to Clive and the Wilkins family.

Lon wasn't normal. He wasn't like other men.

Lon was demanding. Primitive. Uncompromising.

He did as he pleased and he expected everyone else to do what he wanted, too.

"I need to go see to the guests," she said tautly, hanging on to her tattered pride. "Since you're determined to stay I hope you'll enjoy yourself. And when you're ready to go, you know your way out."

Lon walked out of the library, through the large paneled doors, aware that she was still watching him.

His lips twisted, rather amused that even after all these years Sophie still underestimated him so much. It made him realize how little she'd ever known him.

While Clive proposed to Sophie, Lon had backed off, given her up, tried his best to forget he'd ever loved her, but Clive was gone and no longer standing between them.

No one was standing between them. Not even the fiercely controlling Countess Wilkins who, having lost her only child, had put her talons into her daughter-in-law.

Alonso turned at the entrance to the grand salon and walked through the crowds thronging the ballroom entrance. Through the tall arched windows silver white moonlight bathed pale antique pots spilling over with white French tulips.

Alonso felt a stab of nostalgia. The late Earl should be here.

For nearly fifteen years the Earl had headed up Bank of England's Latin America division and the Wilkins had lived in numerous South American countries—Ecuador, Chile, Colombia, Brazil—and the Countess hated them all. When the Earl retired, leaving his senior position with Bank of England, the Wilkins finally returned to England and Countess Wilkins was able to embrace all things English and expensive.

Boxwood and laurels, in. Bird of paradise, out.

Rose and white chintz, in. Rattan and Colonial, out.

Shepherd's pie, in. Grilled beef, out.

Proper English girls, in. International and American expats, out.

Lon turned to the bar alongside the tall multipaned windows, the windows dressed in rose, red, and gold striped silk and tied with fat gold tassels. "Gin and tonic," he said, giving the bartender his order.

A blonde in pale pink silk leaned past him. She was tall and long-limbed and exceptionally beautiful. "Make that two," she said, shooting Alonso a small, sly smile.

Lord Lindley's daughter Amanda. "Hello, Manda."

"Why don't you ever call me?" she asked, turning to face him.

"Because I'm too old for you," he answered, handing her the cocktail she'd requested.

"Hardly. Even if you were, you're disgustingly gorgeous, Lon. And you know I want you to call."

"I don't have your number."

"Well, I have yours. So I guess I'll call you."

He laughed softly. Times had changed. Women had changed. Today they knew what they wanted and they went for it. Unapologetically. "Your father would never approve."

Her eyebrows arched. "Yes he would. He knows you're a hell of a businessman, and he knows I fancy you like mad."

"Which means he believes I can afford you."

"Well, you can, can't you?"

He picked up his glass but he wasn't really thirsty. His thoughts weren't even on Manda, but on Sophie who'd appeared in the ballroom entrance in her gorgeous red gown, and she wasn't alone.

Federico Alvare was here. Just as he'd said.

What balls, Lon thought. Alvare had balls. Which meant that Sophie was indeed in danger.

Alvare had phoned Alonso last night. "Heard you were back in England and visiting at Melrose Court," Alvare had said. "Did you enjoy your dinner with Lady and Countess Wilkins?"

Alvare had to have spies, or he was personally following Sophie. Either way Lon knew he had to stay close. He couldn't let Alvare hurt Sophie the way he'd hurt Clive. "Stay away from her," Lon said, battling the icy deadliness inside him.

"Still jealous?" Federico mocked. "You were always so jealous of Lord Wilkins. Now you're jealous of me."

"I'm not jealous of you. I know who you are. I know what you are—"

"Be careful," Federico interrupted softly, all laughter gone. "I know you don't want her hurt."

"What do you want?"

"Come to the Wilkins' ball. Maybe I'll tell you."

Hatred filled Lon. "You're attending the ball?"

"Of course. I'm Lady Wilkins' special guest." Federico laughed again, a short harsh laugh, and hung up.

CHAPTER FOUR

JAW clenched, Alonso watched Federico and Sophie circle the ballroom. Federico's hand rested on Sophie's waist, and his dark head inclined, as if listening intently to every word she said.

Lon's gut tightened. He'd kill Alvare if he kept touching Sophie.

Manda placed a hand on Lon's sleeve. "You're so wicked! You're not even listening to me," she pouted.

Amanda was right. He wasn't listening to Amanda. He was too busy keeping an eye on Federico as the man's hand moved up and down Sophie's back. "I'm sorry, Manda," Lon apologized, "there's someone I must speak with. Please excuse me."

On the other side of the ballroom, Sophie's heart raced. Federico hadn't stopped touching her since he arrived a half hour ago and her skin crawled each time he put his hand on her. She wanted to shake him off, wanted to ask him to keep his distance but she couldn't afford to alienate him. He was her ticket to Brazil—literally—and she knew he had information about Clive's death.

Stay calm, she told herself. Don't let him know you're uncomfortable. It won't be long until you're in Brazil.

Just as Federico cornered her by the towering Christmas tree, Alonso appeared at their side.

"A brilliant party, Sophie," Alonso said, leaning down to kiss her cheek before turning to Federico. "I'm surprised to see you here. Didn't think this was your kind of event."

Federico looked Lon up and down. "I don't think

we've met before.'' He extended his hand. ''Federico Alvare.''

Not met? Lon's lip nearly curled. Oh, they'd met. They'd met several times actually, the last looking down the barrel of a gun. ''We've met,'' Lon retorted. ''We've had a number of…conversations.''

Federico shook his head. ''Afraid not. You must be thinking of someone else. We South Americans look alike to you English.''

Lon felt Federico's amusement. ''I'm South American, too. My father's family is from Buenos Aires.''

''But your accent is so English.''

Lon forced himself to smile even though his pulse was accelerating. ''A product of my boarding school years,'' he answered evenly, fighting the urge to grab Alvare by the throat and tear him apart, limb from limb. ''So what brings you to England?''

''Christmas shopping,'' Federico answered smiling. ''And a chance to escort Lady Wilkins to Sao Paulo for the New Year.'' He shot Sophie a warm look. ''We're going to have a wonderful trip, aren't we?''

She turned pale. ''It'll be a good chance to see where Clive did business.'' Her voice sounded hoarse. ''Señor Alvare's been kind enough to secure me the services of an excellent private investigator.''

Lon scraped his molars across each other. ''How kind.'' He reached for Sophie's hand. ''May I have a word with you, *muñeca?*''

He didn't even wait for her to respond. With her hand in his, he tugged her after him, feeling her cold fingers clench in protest. They exited through the brocade covered door used by the caterers, passed through the servants hall, down toward the kitchen.

''Where are we going?'' she hissed.

''Somewhere we can talk.''

"I thought we'd just about covered every topic possible."

The large kitchen was crowded with staff and visiting caterers but Lon found Sophie a chair at the enormous farm table in the corner by the stone hearth. "Sit. *Please.*"

He turned to one of the catering staff. "Coffee. Two, please. One black and one with milk and sugar."

Then he stripped off his tuxedo jacket and draped it across her bare shoulders. "You're mad to even contemplate a trip to Harrod's with Alvare, much less a trip to Brazil. He's bad news, Sophie. He can't even keep his hands off you."

"And what's this?" she asked, indicating the coat he was settling around her. "Armor to keep him away?"

"I'd give you a chastity belt if I thought it'd help."

His words sent a ripple through her and she shivered. Suddenly grateful for the jacket, Sophie pulled the lapels closer, glancing from him to the cheerful fire burning next to them. "That's medieval."

"It's civilized compared to what I want to do to you."

Her head turned and she stared him down. "You don't own me."

"I don't want to own you. I just want you safe."

Implying she wasn't safe with Federico. But would she be any safer with Alonso?

Lon put a foot on one of the rails of her chair, drawing her chair even closer to his. "Would you like a background report on your friend?"

"No."

"He's into drugs, Sophie. Serious drugs. Dangerous drugs."

"How do you know?" she asked, acutely aware of Lon's close proximity, the strength of his thigh, the warmth of his body. She wrapped her hands around the coffee cup placed before her. "And what does he do with the drugs? Smuggles?" She saw his eyes narrow. She'd guessed right. "Really, Alonso, that's an awful stereotype coming from you."

Lon felt his lips curl, torn between irony and worry. "Sophie, if you want to go to Brazil, let me take you. I know Brazil. I have safe places we can stay. Friends who'll watch out for you."

She looked down and he saw how she struggled with her emotions, and he saw anger and pain flicker across her elegant features one after the other. But then she lifted her head and her cool, clear gaze met his, the lavender flecks brighter in the glow of firelight. "I appreciate your concern, Alonso. I really do. But this is something I have to do…my way."

"Why?"

Sophie suddenly moved forward, one slender hand touching his white dress shirt.

Lon's body instantly hardened. He glanced from her small hand up to her face. "Do you ever think about us as we…were?" she whispered.

Endlessly, he thought, wanting to cup her cheek, caress her skin with his thumb. "Now and then."

"You and Clive were such good friends." Her voice, young and unconsciously yearning, seemed to float in the warmth of the kitchen. She glanced past his shoulder to the bustle of uniformed staff. "We did have fun once, didn't we?"

"The fun times aren't over, Sophie."

Her shoulders lifted. "Clive's *dead*."

"Yes, darling, but you aren't."

Her face crumpled and she tried to stand, but he reached out for her, clasping her arm, holding her still. "What's happening inside your head, Sophie? Tell me what you're thinking…tell me what you're trying to do."

She shook her head, one painful emotion after another flickering over her features. "I did something awful, Lon. I can't even tell you—"

His heart stilled. His body turned to stone.

Don't let her be involved with Valdez.

Don't let her be tangled in Clive's mess...

He steeled himself. Even if she did something awful, he wouldn't lose her. "Nothing's happened that can't be undone."

"That's not true." Slowly she slid his coat off and handed it back to him. "I better get back to the guests."

"Federico," he said bitterly.

Her expression looked grieved. "You've got to stop this, Lon. You're just going to drive me away—"

Lon swore. Violently. "Dammit, Sophie! Why are you so blind? Why can't you see what's right before you?"

She swallowed with difficulty and the red silk gown with the daring décolleté rose and fell with her shallow breath. "You have to trust me, Lon."

His chest felt tight and tender at the same time. "No, *you* have to trust *me*. There are things I know, Sophie, that you don't know. Places I've been that you can't even imagine—"

"Sophie!" Countess Wilkins bustled into the kitchen, interrupting Lon. "I've been looking *everywhere* for you. Lady Halverson is beside herself. Apparently she can't find her stole. The chinchilla. Light gray—"

"Yes, I remember," Sophie said.

"I knew you would." Louisa breathed a sigh of relief. "And I told her you'd know right where it was. Come quickly and help her locate it before she upsets any guests. You know how theatrical she is."

Sophie's gaze met Lon's. "Yes, indeed."

The Countess rushed out and Sophie pushed away from the table. "Duty calls."

Lon reached for her hand. "Promise me you won't do anything stupid."

She smiled wryly. "That's an awfully big promise."

His gaze never wavered from hers. "Don't get on a plane with Alvare. Don't let him make travel plans for you. If you have to go to Brazil—"

She suddenly leaned over and pressed a kiss to his cheek. "Thank you," she whispered. "For still caring. And for wanting the best for me. I do appreciate it. More than you know."

Lon watched her disappear from the kitchen and he stayed where he was, fighting the urge to go after her, fearing for her already.

God, she was still so innocent. She didn't realize that there was a whole nasty world out there that could seduce a good man in no time flat.

She had no idea just how dark Clive's world had become. How was he supposed to protect her from the truth about Clive? How was he supposed to protect her from Valdez, Alvare...*himself?*

Who the hell did he think he was? Then he heard Sophie's voice echo in his head. *You're like Superman, Lon.*

Superman. Right.

In the grand entry, Federico waited while Sophie said goodbyes to Lord and Lady Halverson. As the door closed behind the couple, Federico took her elbow. "What did he say to you?"

Sophie sighed. This was getting so complicated. "He doesn't want me to go with you."

Federico searched her face. "Why not?"

She swallowed. "He thinks I'd be...better off...going with him. He says he has friends in Brazil—"

"Yes, but what kind of friends?" Federico put his

hands on her shoulders. He was a good head shorter than Alonso and when he bent his head a little he looked easily into her eyes. "I guarantee his friends won't know what my man in Sao Paulo knows. His friends won't have the information you want."

She nodded wearily. All she wanted to do was go upstairs and take off this red gown and slip into something comfy and warm.

"If you're worried about being harassed by him, we can always leave early in the morning. There's a 6:00 a.m. flight to Sao Paulo. We don't have to wait until after the holidays."

She lifted her head, looked at him. "But…nothing's packed."

"So you go upstairs in a little while, and finish packing. Then I'll return for you early in the morning, around four. We'll take the first flight out in the morning."

"You think so?"

"I know so. Our tickets are first class. There won't be any problem moving our departure forward by a few days, especially as we have our visas all in order."

She saw Alonso appear in the doorway. Lon's narrowed eyes swept them, and she could see how he saw them— Sophie and Federico alone together, with Federico's hands on her bare shoulders.

Lon wasn't going to disappear. He wasn't going to let Sophie leave the country without tagging along himself,…on the same plane. She made a quick decision. "Let's do it. Let's go first thing in the morning."

Lon drove home from the party with the nagging sense that he'd screwed up royally by leaving Sophie behind at Melrose Court.

He didn't trust her. She should be under surveillance

twenty-four, seven. If he could have, he would have taken her home with him tonight, daring red ballgown and all.

She'd be safe with him.

Well, she'd *be* with him. Safe was questionable. He still wanted her and she wasn't exactly turned off him. No, she wasn't turned off at all.

But she was nervous around him. Jittery.

Something was eating at her, and that something had to do with Clive and Federico and Brazil.

Lon pulled into his garage, sat a moment with his headlights shining on the wall.

He was missing something. It was right here, in front of his nose, but he was still missing it. Lon growled deep in his throat, frustrated. He felt as if he was groping in the dark and he hated feeling stupid.

Sophie could not have found Federico Alvare on her own. He had to have come to her…but why would Alvare do that? Lon shifted into park, turned off the engine, impatiently drummed the steering wheel. And Alvare hadn't been secretive about contacting Sophie. That's what made Lon's skin crawl.

Why would Alvare, a man wanted by governments on several continents, publicly meet with Sophie, wining and dining her, when he had to know he—they—were being watched?

When he had to know that his lunch dates with Lady Wilkins, the wife of a man accused of betraying his country, would create tremendous suspicion?

Because Federico Alvare wanted to draw attention to himself.

He *wanted* the Secret Service to know.

He wanted *Lon* to know. And what better way to get the MI6's attention, and Lon's attention, than to move into Lon's backyard…and move in on Lon's woman.

Lon headed into the house and stripping off his tuxedo

he stepped into the shower, trying to clear his head, trying to see what else was happening here.

He had to figure it out before Sophie got on that plane for Sao Paulo because Brazil would be a disaster—not just for her, but for him.

It'd been a bloodbath the night it all came down in Sao Paulo. Six men died—Clive, the two U.K. agents, and three of Miguel Valdez's men including Valdez's younger brother. Only Lon had walked away. Well, walked away was a bit of misnomer. Lon had been rushed by helicopter medics to the nearest emergency room. He was still in the hospital when Sophie called asking for his help.

Despite still being woozy on his feet, he'd checked himself out of the hospital and returned to England for Clive's funeral.

Sophie had never even known he was hurt. He didn't mention his injury, or his pain, and when he collapsed later that night and was rushed back into surgery for internal bleeding, he insisted that no one tell her. She had enough to worry about. She didn't need to worry about him.

Lon was asleep, dreaming about that last night in Sao Paulo, when the computer in the adjoining room started beeping and printing pages.

Alonso sat up, grabbed his clock. Six a.m. He knew the beeping was the Global Positioning System he'd planted in the back of Sophie's wireless phone the night he'd had dinner at Melrose Court.

The computer was telling him that Sophie had just left England.

At five-twenty that morning, Sophie and Federico had boarded the British Airways flight to Sao Paulo. At precisely six a.m. the Boeing 777 left the ground.

As the huge Boeing jet rapidly climbed, Sophie settled back in her seat, tried to calm her butterflies. In a couple hours Louisa would wake to discover the note from Sophie explaining she'd gone with friends for the Christmas holiday. Later in the day Lon would probably call Melrose Court to check in on her. By the time he phoned—and discovered she'd gone—there'd be nothing he could do.

Ten hours later Sophie and Federico cleared customs in Sao Paulo and then hailed a cab for their hotel.

The hotel manager greeted them personally when they checked in. "We've reserved a lovely room for you," he said to Sophie, bowing over her hand. "One of our nicest suites."

Sophie's white on white suite was indeed luxurious— the only color present was in the stark zebra skins scattered on the floor and a tall red vase on the coffee table overflowing with red roses, red tulips and red Gerber daisies.

There was music on and the song playing took her way back. The tune hadn't ever been a favorite of hers, but it'd been wildly popular when she and Clive were newlyweds. Sophie quickly snapped the stereo off.

Federico's suite was next to hers, and he stopped by a few minutes after the bell captain departed to see if she was ready to head downstairs to explore the city.

Head out now? Impossible. Sophie pleaded exhaustion and said she really needed a nap first.

"You don't want to nap now," Federico answered, crossing her room and pulling open the white curtains. "It's morning here now. You must get adjusted to the time difference, and the best way to do that is to keep moving. We've a busy day planned. Señor Chebe, the investigator I've hired, is meeting us downstairs in just a few minutes."

Señor Chebe was a short stout man with a huge smile and a warm, friendly handshake. "You speak Portugese," he said.

"Not much," Sophie answered, still swaying a bit on her feet. Maybe Federico didn't need rest, but she was dying to stretch out and close her eyes. "I'm better with Spanish, but even that's quite rusty."

"Then we'll stay with English, *Señora*. I'm not very good, but I shall try." He led Sophie and Federico outside to the brilliant summer sunshine.

Although it was only midmorning the temperature was already quickly rising.

A black sedan was waiting for them in the drive. Señor Chebe slid behind the steering wheel and Federico and Sophie sat in the back seat. She'd hoped Federico was going to ride in front with Señor Chebe.

"Did you ever meet my husband?" she asked, leaning forward to speak to Señor Chebe.

"No," he answered, pulling away from the curb. "But I'd heard of him. I knew he'd worked for the Bank of England, in their Latin America division. I knew he handled government and institutional accounts in Brazil."

Sophie flexed her fingers. "The people I'm to see on my trip—do any of them work for the Bank of England?"

"No."

"Don't you think we should try to meet with people from the bank?"

Señor Chebe glanced back at her. "I do not think those people will get you the information you want, *Señora*."

The city traffic was already thick by eight, and it took them nearly a half hour to wind through the enormous metropolitan downtown and reach the outskirts of Sao Paulo. In the outskirts of the city, Señor Chebe pulled into a small executive airport.

"Are we picking someone up?" she asked when he parked and pocketed the keys.

"We're taking a plane to Iguazu Falls," Federico answered with a glance at his watch.

"But we don't have any luggage—"

"You won't need any, Sophie."

A day trip? To Iguazu. "What are we gong to do at the falls?"

Federico smiled down at her as he assisted her from the back of the car. "Iguazu is where it all began."

But Federico was wrong, she discovered hours later. Dead wrong. Iguazu wasn't the beginning. Iguazu was the end.

CHAPTER FIVE

HOURS into the worst nightmare of her life, Sophie crouched in the corner of the hut, her tiny wireless phone gripped tightly in her hand, *Answer, answer, Alonso, you have to be there. You have to answer.*

But Lon didn't pick up. Just his voice mail came on.

Sophie hung up. Beads of perspiration slid down her back, between her breasts, beneath the weight of her heavy hair, and yet on the inside she was icy cold. Freezing.

Shaking, she stared at the phone, wondered who else she could call, wondering if there was anyone else who would know what to do. Because Alonso would know what to do. If anyone could reach her now, it'd be him.

She dialed his number again, ignoring the pinch of a flying insect as it landed on her sticky bare arm. The subtropics were full of bugs. She'd never liked the bugs. Never liked the jungle. Why, oh why, had she come back here now?

Clive.

But she couldn't think of him now. He certainly couldn't help her now and she concentrated on the periodic static on the line. Finally the number connected, rang a half dozen times and Lon's voice mail picked up again.

She didn't hang up this time. "Lon, it's me, Sophie. I'm in trouble, big trouble—" she broke off as a shout sounded outside. Someone was coming.

She froze and for a split second Sophie felt like stone, utterly still as she strained to hear every noise, every voice. The warm dense humid heat wrapped her and she tasted fear in her mouth. Her senses had never been so keen, her nerves stretched taut, awake, alive. The instinct for self-preservation was so strong. It drove every pulse, every thought, every breath.

Swallowing the raw sour fear she pressed the phone closer to her lips. "I'm in Brazil, Lon, and they took me near the border, not far from the Iguaza Falls. They shot Señor Chebe, and I'm not sure about Federico, but it's bad, Lon. Very bad."

She jerked at the sound of gunfire outside her hut, exhaling in a thin rush of air.

After they'd ambushed her car, the men had dragged everyone from the vehicle. Nelo Chebe had protested and someone shot him.

Then they had blindfolded her, bundling her into the back of what appeared to be a tarp covered truck. The jolting truck ride seemed to last forever. It could have been just a half hour. It could have been longer. Time stopped, and without her vision, she had no point of reference.

Now footsteps sounded outside her door and Sophie's heart jumped wildly. She slammed the phone closed and her gaze swept the small hut, taking in the narrow metal cot with an even narrower mattress, her purse which had been dumped in the corner of her room, ransacked by her captors, the metal bowl on the floor in the opposite corner.

Where could she hide the phone? What to do with the phone? She dove toward the cot, sliding the small wireless phone between it's metal springs and mattress even as her door thrust open.

Seeing the door open, Sophie scrambled backward and tripped on the cot. Her legs gave way and she sat down heavily, her narrow skirt skewed high on her thigh.

Men pushed into her hut. There were several of them. Many of them. Three, four, bunched together. She felt rather than saw them look at her, look at her long disheveled hair, and look even longer at her pale, bare thigh. Her fingers itched to pull the skirt hem down but she wouldn't give the soldiers—or guerillas, or whatever they were—the satisfaction.

She wasn't going to be afraid.

She wasn't going to cower. She was Lady Sophie Wilkins, wife of Clive Wilkins, and she sat taller, drawing her spine stiff as if lifted by a string from her top vertebrae.

"You said you were American," the man in the front said, no machine gun across his chest, just a belt with two holsters—including two black pistols—and a sheath replete with knife.

He stood with his hands on his hips and Sophie felt the weight of his narrowed gaze. She felt the weight of all their eyes. There were just three men, she saw now, but the collective, unblinking weight of their gaze felt impossibly heavy.

"I am American."

"Where is your passport?"

"I didn't bring it with me."

"Why not?"

Sophie inhaled, exhaled, drawing the air in and out. Quietly. Calmly. Very calmly. *Do nothing to provoke them. Do nothing to create fresh tension.* "I didn't know I'd need it."

"Where were you born?" the man demanded.

"Omaha. Nebraska."

"But you sound English. Your accent is English."

So someone had finally appreciated her diction classes Countess Wilkins insisted Sophie take before the wedding. "I've lived in England for nearly ten years now."

He pulled a small notebook and broken pencil from his back pocket. "Your married name is Wilkins?"

"Yes."

He wrote this down. "Your maiden name?"

"Johnson." He wrote this down, too, and she dug her nails into her palms, barely feeling the pinch of pain. Sophie Johnson, American. Midwesterner. Yank.

Outsider.

"You've given up your American citizenship?" the man persisted.

The man's English was good. Very very good. "No. But my husband is English, which is why I live in England."

"Is your passport issued by the U.S. or U.K. government?"

"The U.S., but I live in England," she repeated firmly. She hadn't lived in America since her seventh birthday. She hadn't felt American in years. She'd lived too long in other countries, spent too many years ignoring, denying her Midwest roots. "My home is in Somerset."

The man continued to scribble notes to himself. "You said your husband was English."

She felt a flicker of fear, the trepidation back. "Yes."

"And where is your husband now?"

Her heart constricted painfully. For a moment she couldn't breathe and she felt absolutely, totally empty. In that second Sophie realized she had nothing left, nothing but her name and her perfect, aristocratic posture. "Home."

"Somerset?"

"Yes."

The man nodded slowly, almost thoughtfully. "And your husband, Señora Wilkins, what is his first name?"

Her throat sealed closed. She couldn't breathe. Couldn't speak. She stared helplessly at the thickly built man with the equally thick black mustache. The mustache curled around his lips, not quite a handlebar, but strong, dominant, almost cruel.

The man smiled humorously, lips twisting as if they were sharing a good laugh. ''You can't have forgotten his name already.''

Already? What did he mean by that?

Her head lifted and her gaze met his. But the humor twisting his lips didn't reach his eyes. No, his eyes splintered ice. There was something cold in his eyes, something almost…dead…and she shivered, a real shiver, a shiver she couldn't hide.

And he saw it.

He smiled bigger. And the cold flat darkness in his eyes seemed to fill his face.

''His name, *Señora?*''

''Clive,'' she whispered, her voice failing, her courage failing, her world coming apart.

''An unusual name.''

Her eyes filled with tears and she silently cursed herself, hating that she'd shown weakness, hating even more that she'd shown emotion. ''An English name.''

''For a proper English lord.'' How did he know that? How did he know that Clive was connected, an aristocrat? How *could* he know?

The three men left the hut, closing the door behind them, and yet for long minutes Sophie didn't move, her thoughts tangled.

The man's words rang in her head, haunting her. *A proper English lord.*

Lord Clive Wilkins.

Maybe it was just a joke. Maybe the soldier was trying to be funny, poking at the famous stiff upper lip of the English.

But she didn't know for certain, and she couldn't—

wouldn't—ask. All she knew was that she was most definitely in a very bad place.

Sophie had never known time to pass so slowly. But now it was finally growing dark and shadows stretched across the dirt floor. She'd been waiting for the shadows, waiting for a little cover before retrieving her phone from between the cot spring and mattress. Thank God they hadn't found her phone. They'd checked her purse thoroughly, patted her down, but hadn't discovered the credit card slim wireless phone in the pocket of her light traveling coat.

Trembling, Sophie hit redial on her phone, even as some crawling insect bit her ankle. She smashed the insect and prayed for Lon to answer. This time he did.

"Alonso!" Her voice broke and suddenly she couldn't make another sound, not even that of the agonized sob wrenching her insides.

"*Sophie.*"

His voice sounded terse, rough, like that of the emerald mine he'd once worked and now owned.

"Lon, they've accused me of smuggling. Drugs, I think it's drugs. I can't be sure. The interrogations lasted for hours. It looks quite bad for me—" she broke off, fatigue and fear deepening her voice.

"No one will hurt you, Sophie."

"But they shot Señor Chebe."

"No one will hurt you," he repeated.

"Oh, Alonso, I'm in such trouble."

It was the first time in two years that he'd heard panic in her voice. Even at Clive's funeral, Sophie had managed to be calm, composed, but now she sounded real, and positively frantic.

"Where are you?" he asked, zipping closed his duffel bag, glancing out at the ground which loomed ever closer.

They'd be landing soon. Ten minutes, fifteen minutes at the most.

"Somewhere near the falls, or along the river. I still hear water," she answered faintly.

Lon scanned the dark mass of land below. There were few lights. The rain forest stretched in all directions, covering hundreds of miles, connecting Uruguay, Brazil, Argentina and Paraguay.

He'd boarded his jet early that morning, just a couple hours after Sophie's departure. During the flight he'd spread his work out on the table, turned on his computer, and logged on to the satellite network, checking Sophie's location. Thanks to the battery-operated GPS he'd planted in her wireless phone—about the only smart thing he'd done so far—he was able to pinpoint her exact location.

Valdez' men were holding her in a remote, and heavily forested location, just north of the falls.

It wouldn't be an easy rescue. But he'd done worse. "Good. That helps," he told her.

She inhaled, once, twice, shallow, panicked breaths. "I would have gone with them, Lon. They didn't have to shoot Señor Chebe—"

"Tell me about Chebe."

"He was my guide…my private investigator. He's the one I wired the money to."

No, he thought. She didn't wire money to Chebe. She'd wired money to Federico's bank account in Brazil. If Chebe was being paid, he was being paid by Federico.

"They would have never asked you to go with them," he said. "They never ask. The men who took you, their methods are violent. It's about intimidation. You know that." He spoke calmly, unemotionally, as if they were discussing the weather or the market volatility. It was important she keep a level head. He needed her to help buy him time. "For all we know Chebe could have been working for them—"

"So why would they shoot him if he were one of them?"

"To make an impression—which they did. To show you they're serious—which they are."

She'd run out of words and for a moment the only sound was that of her crying, soft muffled tears that shredded him on the inside, tears that made him seethe and burn.

Clive had done this.

Clive had created this.

And Clive wasn't even around to clean up after his own damn mess.

He kept his fury from his voice. "Anything else you can tell me about your surroundings, Sophie? Or your captors?"

"There's quite a few of them," she answered huskily, "and I don't think things are going so well around here. There's lots of shouting. They've been shouting almost all afternoon. Gunfire, too." She hesitated. "How could they think I'm involved with drugs?"

He had a pretty damn good idea, but he wasn't about to break the news over the phone. Some things were best said in person. "So they've tried to talk to you?"

"They were asking some questions a couple of hours ago." Her voice thickened, dropped lower. "They asked about Clive."

He said nothing.

"I think they know who he is, Lon. I think they knew who I was when they took me."

Of course they did. Clive had started to work for Valdez and Alvare. Federico had recruited him. "I need some time, Sophie. Probably twenty-four hours. Do you understand what I'm saying?" He wouldn't need that long but in case something did go wrong he didn't want her worrying.

"Twenty-four hours," she repeated numbly.

She made it sound light-years away. Right now it felt light-years away. Lon knew a hell of a lot could happen between now and then.

"I'm scared, Alonso."

He closed his eyes, seeing her against his mind's eye, her long silky black hair, her serious blue eyes. Clive hadn't deserved her. He'd never appreciated her, understood her. "Don't be afraid, Sophie. When you wake up in the morning, know that I'll be nearby. Even if you can't see me, I'll be close to you, watching over you. Nothing will happen to you."

"But if it does—"

"It won't," he cut off unmercifully. He had contacts all over the world, including Argentina. These were people he'd worked with many times, people who'd protect Sophie at all cost. Three of his best contacts were already in Iguazu. Lon had e-mailed Sophie's location to them and knew they'd intervene quickly if need be.

"Just give me a day." His voice was firm, commanding. "Half a day. One night. That's all I ask."

"Okay." Her answer was weak, subdued.

"*Sophie.*"

"Yes?"

"I'll see you soon."

The Gulfstream landed without a bump and Lon gathered his duffel bag and computer equipment. Iguazu lay 800 miles north of Buenos Aires, and the new airport catered primarily to the tourists flocking to visit the falls, but no commercial jets were scheduled to land until morning and Lon reached the street curb in record time.

A Jeep and driver were waiting. "Welcome back,

Alonso," the driver said, stepping from the Jeep. An American, he spoke with a hint of a Texas twang, and like Lon, he was somewhere in his early thirties, fit, tan, an advertisement for healthy living.

Lon moved forward to shake Flip's hand. "Good to see you again." Flip and Lon had served together on a joint mission between the CIA and MI6 and the two had become good friends fast. Flip had retired from the CIA about the same time Lon resigned from the MI6. While Lon turned his attention to his emerald mine, Flip had started his own security business, which meant he was qualified to do anything and everything all over the globe. And he did.

Lon tossed his duffel bag into the back of the Jeep and Flip climbed back behind the steering wheel. "Have all the boys arrived?" he asked, taking a seat.

"We're ready," Flip answered, starting the vehicle.

Lon shot Flip a swift glance. "It could be messy."

Flip laughed once, low and mocking. "When isn't it?"

Less than a half hour later, Flip pulled into the parking lot at the big modern hotel overlooking the falls from the Argentina side.

"Your key," Flip said, handing Lon an envelope. "Your room's ready. You wanted a suite. It's on the top floor, the penthouse. You're registered under Galván." Flip was what the department called a Backstop, a person who could vouch for Lon if a target started asking questions about Alonso's alias.

"Thanks."

"So how much does she know?" Flip asked.

Lon swung his duffel bag out of the back. "Not much."

"Anything about your Secret Service background?"

"No."

"About the Galváns?"

"No."

"About your drug enforcement duties?"

"No."

Flip studied Lon. "When did you figure out they'd taken her to get to you?"

"Not until she called."

Flip whistled. "She was bait. From the beginning. They take her and wait for you to follow."

"They knew I'd follow." Lon's smile was lopsided, self-effacing. "I'd follow her to hell if I had to."

"Don't go in tomorrow. Let us do it."

"No way I'm leaving this to you."

Flip leaned on the steering wheel. "We can do it."

"That's not the point. If anything goes wrong, I have to be there. If anything happens to her, I—" he broke off, "I'm there."

Flip nodded. "Then I'll see you in the morning."

"Early."

In his suite Lon showered, shaved, and stretched out on his bed to get a few precious hours sleep. He'd be leaving the hotel and meeting with the boys at three forty-five, and if all went as planned, he'd be with Sophie by four-thirty, and in the safe spot by dawn.

If all went as planned.

Three hours later, the alarm went off, and after dressing, Lon left his open duffel bag teaming with holiday clothes, rainforest maps, and cartons of Kodak film on the foot of his bed.

He was, after all, on holiday.

Two and a half miles away, Sophie shook with fear, and her blouse clung to her like a second skin.

They'd been back. The men. The three from before, and this time, there was a new one with them. Federico Alvare.

She'd stared at Federico for a moment, thinking he'd

come to get her out, but when he stood by the others and just looked at her, no expression on his face, no smile, no sign of recognition, she realized that this whole thing had been orchestrated by him.

"You're one of them," she whispered.

"They work for me," Federico corrected. "These are my...soldiers."

She couldn't believe it. Couldn't believe Lon was so right and she'd been so wrong. Couldn't believe she'd fallen for Federico's sympathy and charm. "You shot Nelo Chebe," she said, finding her voice. "You killed your own man."

Federico shrugged. "He let us down."

"When?"

"That's not really any of your concern, is it, Lady Wilkins?" Federico's warmth was gone, leaving him eerily chilling. "Tell me, did your phone work here in the rainforest? Any problems with the connection?"

Sophie couldn't answer.

"We know you had the phone," Federico continued, his lips curved in a cold, bitter smile. "We left it with you intentionally. Did you make the calls you wanted to make?"

She still couldn't speak, her skin clammy, her body miserably hot and cold at the same time.

"Where is the phone now?" He took a threatening step toward her. "Do not be stupid. Give me the phone."

She pointed to her cot. Federico walked to the cot, lifted the mattress, found the phone. He turned the phone on and clicked through the list of calls made. "How is our good friend, Señor Galván?" he asked, looking at her.

"I don't know who you're talking about."

Federico cocked his head. "You don't know Alonso Galván?"

Alonso Galván? "No."

"The man at the party. The one you've been phoning." He smiled. "That is Alonso Galván."

"No. He's not Galván. He's Alonso Huntsman."

"Huntsman isn't his real name. It's an alias."

She felt so sick on the inside, so scared. Huntsman wasn't an alias. It was Lon's real name. He'd been Huntsman as long as she'd known him. "What do you want with me?"

Federico pocketed the phone. "Nothing."

She stared at him, needing to make sense of this craziness and unable to piece any of it together. "I don't understand."

He pulled a knife. "Then let me spell it out."

She jumped back as Federico moved toward her. Her fear made his smile widen and he crouched in front of her, hands on his knees, his pocketknife in one fist. Sophie found it nearly impossible to look away from the knife but she forced her gaze up, little by little until she saw nothing but Federico's brown eyes.

"You…" he drawled slowly "…are…nothing." His gaze held hers. A cruel smile flickered at his mouth. "You…mean…*nothing*. Poof," he snapped his fingers. "You're gone."

"Then why did you bring me here?"

Her whisper floated between them. Federico's dark eyes gleamed. "I want Galván. Huntsman. Whatever you want to call him. He and I have some unresolved…business. So, tell me. When is he going to be here?"

Federico wanted Alonso. Federico was going to hurt Alonso. Tears filled her eyes. She shook her head.

Federico lifted his knife, grabbed her ponytail. "The truth. *Now*."

She blinked. A tear spilled. "Tomorrow night."

"Tomorrow night?"

She nodded.

"Why tomorrow night?"

Sophie wanted to throw up. "I don't know. He just said he needed twenty-four hours. Just to give him twenty-four hours and he'd be here."

"Thank you, Lady Wilkins. Your cooperation is much appreciated."

Federico stood, pocketed the knife, and the men left.

CHAPTER SIX

SOPHIE slowly slid to the floor, her legs like jelly, unable to hold her up.

Lon had been right. He and Federico had met. Federico knew him. Worse, Federico *wanted* him. And Federico had used her to get to Lon.

She swallowed hard, her limbs shaking with fear and fatigue, even as she sweated profusely, her body unused to the rain forest's cloying heat.

Half shivering, half sweating she tipped her head back against the cot and stared into space. Federico had told her he'd used to work with Clive, so how did that involve Lon? How would Federico have known Lon? Why would he care about Lon? It didn't make sense.

Unless…unless Clive and Lon had been involved in some kind of business deal, something that wasn't altogether legitimate, something that neither of them would want her to know about.

What had they gotten mixed up in? And why was Lon keeping it a secret even now? For that matter, what was Lon's real name? How could he be a Huntsman and Galván?

The thoughts chased around and around in her head. She'd had nothing to eat since arriving and just a little fruit juice to drink. She was hungry. Tired. Scared. And really, really confused.

Head aching, she closed her eyes, relaxing her tired brain. It would be okay, she told herself, it would. Lon was tough. Lon was smart. Lon wouldn't walk into something like this blind…

"Sophie."

The voice was but a whisper but she jerked awake anyway. A man crouched above her and she slammed her head against the edge of the cot trying to escape. "Ouch!"

"Sssh, Sophie, you have to be quiet."

She stopped struggling, fighting to see him through the dark gloom. "Lon?"

"It's me, love."

She felt him cup her cheek and she grabbed his hand. His hand was hard, calloused, his skin warm. Lon. He was real. She wasn't dreaming.

"You're here." She threw herself into his arms, burying her face against his shoulder, her arms wrapping around him, clenching. "You're not supposed to be here yet." Her arms squeezed tighter, muscles locking. She felt the hardness of his body, the thickness of his arms, the curve of bicep. She'd never felt anything half so wonderful in her whole life. "They want you, Lon. They're using me to trap you."

"I know." He pulled her to her feet. "That's why we've got to move fast." He thrust an armful of clothes at her. "Put these on. And hurry."

She stripped off her skirt and creased blouse and pulled on clothes that looked almost black in the dark. Trousers too big at the waist. A cotton T-shirt too snug at the chest. Thank goodness the hiking boots were just the right size. She tied her shoelaces and finished them with a double knot. "Done."

He put a hair elastic in her hand. "Braid it. Knot the braid under. You don't want your hair in the way."

What he meant was he didn't want anyone to recognize her.

She braided her thick hair quickly, trying not to think about what would happen next. "How'd you get here so fast?"

"I made good time."

"Not good. *Amazing.*" She finished twisting the band around her hair, cinching the braid up so it barely showed.

He plonked a dark cap on her head. "You could say I was strongly motivated," he said and she heard the heat and edge of anger in his voice.

Lon held out a vest. "Now put this on."

"What's that?"

"Precautionary measure."

Bulletproof vest, she thought, as he snapped it closed. Sophie swallowed. "Are you wearing one?"

"Yes."

"So you know they have guns."

"Yes."

She touched the tip of her tongue to her very dry lips. "So how do we do this?"

"We're going to walk out."

Her mouth went ever drier. Her legs quaked. She battled a spike of mind-blowing fear. "Just walk out?"

"Do you have a better suggestion?"

"Lon, they have *big* guns."

He patted something on his shoulder. "Me, too." Then he hesitated. "I've got some guys outside and they'll get you out of here. They're armed. They're wearing vests. They know what they need to do."

He motioned for her to open the door and for a moment she couldn't breathe. The panic was back, and a new fear, a fear unlike any other. "You're not coming with me?"

"I'm coming," he answered quietly. "I'm just coming last. In case anything goes wrong, we've established a safe house, and my guys will take you there."

In case anything goes wrong.

He meant, if he got killed.

Her eyes burned and she felt a knot of terror fill her chest. It was all so crazy…so wrong…

She'd dragged him into this. She'd put him in danger. God knows why Federico wanted Lon, but there was definitely bitter blood between them. "Nothing better go wrong," she whispered, grabbing his shirt, fiercely hanging on to him. He had to come through this okay. He had to be okay. She couldn't bear it if anything happened to him.

"Promise me," she choked, "promise me nothing will happen to you."

He didn't answer her and she felt hot tears fill her eyes. The danger overwhelmed her. The danger was real.

She stood on tiptoe, pressed her face up to his. "You're coming with me, understand?"

"I haven't waited this long to lose you now, darling."

His rough voice tore at her heart. "Say it again," she begged.

Instead he lowered his head and kissed her, one hard kiss full of promise and suggestion. Then he lifted his head, brushed her lips with his thumb. "See you soon, *muñeca.*"

Lon stepped away, swatted her on the rear, and opened the door. "Now get going."

Sophie could hardly see through the tears filming her eyes. He was crazy. Absolutely crazy.

Gathering her courage, she pushed through the tent flap and walked out into the still dark night. Two men rose from their crouched positions on either side of the door and buffered her. Lon was right behind.

Quietly they trotted through the sleeping camp and Sophie felt the silence all the way through her. It was too quiet. She was certain eyes were watching. Then out of nowhere gunfire exploded.

"Get her out of here, now!"

Sophie heard Lon's guttural command and a third man appeared from nowhere. She was literally being swept away, completely hidden by the soldiers hired by Lon. How could they see? She felt blind as a bat.

But the men ran, and as they were reaching the edge of the brush she heard a loud pop behind her. Lon swore, a low harsh groan. But he didn't slow, he just kept moving, keeping her back covered and as they pushed deeper into the brush, Lon swung her into his arms. She spotted the goggles he was wearing.

No wonder they could see in the dark. All the men were wearing night vision goggles.

Lon dropped her onto his shoulder and abruptly they separated, one of Lon's men going wide to the left, one cutting to the right, and the last man falling behind to cover Lon.

Eventually Sophie's terror gave way to discomfort. Lon was running and his shoulder was big and hard and jolting relentlessly against her middle and the pack on his back rose and fell, periodically slamming into her face. "Put me down."

"Not a chance." He clamped a hard arm across the back of her thighs, holding her tighter.

Bouncing away on his shoulder, Sophie struggled to not get sick. She closed her eyes, breathe, just breathe normally, she told herself, and then opened her eyes and tried to locate a nonmoving spot on the ground.

It was after opening her eyes the second time she realized the man behind them was no longer there. Had he been hit? Hurt?

Sophie clutched the shoulder on Lon's khaki shirt. "Your guy is gone."

"Good. He was supposed to head for the Jeep."

She lifted her hands to protect herself as a stray branch snapped off in her face. "Why don't we get the Jeep?"

"Because the Jeep is more dangerous."

"I'm not so sure about that."

Sophie suddenly felt a stinging swat across her upended behind. "What's that for?"

"For being a smart mouth. Not following directions." He suddenly stopped, and with a shift of his shoulder, set her on her feet. Lon quickly stripped off the heavy vest, the goggles from around his neck and shoved them in the pack before slinging it onto his shoulders again. "*And* for leaving London without me."

"There were things I had to do on my own. Things I needed to find out—" she broke off, noticing the stain on his shoulder now that the vest was gone. His right sleeve was dark, muddied brown in the dim light penetrating the dense foliage. He *had* been shot. "You're hurt."

"No."

"But your shoulder—"

"Is fine," he finished quickly.

"It looks like blood."

"It's not. Now let's get moving. You don't want your boyfriend Federico catching us." Lon was already charging ahead, half walking, half jogging, bending back branches and gray-green brush for her as he went.

As they pushed on, deeper into the subtropical rain forest, the roar of the falls grew louder. They couldn't be walking to the falls. They had to be walking away. There were no roads near the falls. No escape near the falls.

A yellow-throated toucan with a bright red chest flew past Sophie, black wings almost clipping her face and she nearly screamed.

Lon stopped, turned. "What?"

"A bird," she choked, mopping her brow, her skin clammy with perspiration. "A *big* bird."

He shot a look of disbelief, one black eyebrow arching. "Sophie."

"Yes?"

"Unless it's armed, and about to shoot, please don't do that again." Then he turned around and set off again.

But as they walked, Lon seemed to grow stiffer. His right arm no longer hung naturally against his side, but pressed close against his body.

She was worried about his shoulder. "Lon?"

"I'm really not in the mood to talk."

"But your shoulder—"

He stopped. "Do *not* mention my shoulder again, all right?"

She swallowed hard, her eyes fixed on the big ugly stain on his shoulder where the fabric looked brown in places, purple black in others. He'd bled several times, she thought. The wound seemed to bleed then stop, and then bleed again. "Okay."

They climbed steadily uphill for another hour or so, and again the falls grew louder. After a while the heat felt less intense and the hot stagnant air seemed lighter, cooler.

Suddenly Lon tossed down the heavy pack he'd been carrying and it bounced in the tangled undergrowth. "We're stopping here."

"For how long?" Sophie restlessly paced the small clearing, trying to imagine how long they'd be hanging out in the rain forest before help came. There were trees and shrubs but no real protection and she was already longing for a shower and a comfortable bed.

"Until we're done with breakfast," Lon answered, crouching by his pack, and pulling out small silver foil bags.

She stood over him, watching him sort through the silver pouches. Space age food. Familiar names on the pouches but in weird alien shapes. It was all dehydrated. This was the stuff serious climbers took on long trips. Just how long were they going to be out here anyway?

Lon handed her a handful of packages and she took

them, sitting down and greedily sorting through the three he'd given her. A protein bar, pouch of dehydrated fruit, a fortified beverage. "What happens now?" she asked, trying to decide which packet to open first.

"We eat."

No kidding. She shot him an irritated look. "After. Later. How do we get out of here?"

"We don't. Not for a while."

"But we're still close to them, we're practically sitting under their nose!"

"Exactly. They'll think we've headed away from here and they'll disperse, look for us in town, at the resort hotels, the police station, anywhere but in their backyard."

"No offense, but I'd rather take my odds with the police, or the local embassy."

"Sophie, in case you haven't noticed we're in the middle of nowhere. There's no embassy here. There are three countries bordering these falls and each country has its own police and politics. And in the event that our friend Federico works with one of the governments, I don't want to go public for help."

"What about *our* government?"

He looked at her for a long, hard moment. "What about them?"

She saw a blaze of fire in his eyes and it scared her. Lon was angry with her, more angry than he was letting on. "Why can't we go to our government? We're not in trouble with our government, are we?"

He didn't answer immediately.

"Lon?" She felt a hint of panic.

"I'm not. But you could be."

"Why?"

"Alvare."

Alvare. Her association with Federico Alvare. She'd

been spending time with a man that her government didn't trust. She'd flown here with Federico, checked into a hotel with Federico, put herself in Federico's care. Good God. Imagine what it must look like…

She glanced up, met Lon's gaze. He said nothing, just looked at her, all hulking form and silence. Then his wide jaw tightened, and his blue eyes snapped wide open. But when he spoke, his voice came out deadly quiet. "How intimate have you been with him?"

Her body jerked. "Not at all."

"Yet you left the country with him."

"It's you he wanted," she interrupted tersely. "I know he used me to get to you, but it's you he wanted all along, not me."

"I told you to stay away from him."

Too late, she thought, drawing a small breath. "You said he's into drugs. Smuggling. Is that what you and Clive were involved in, too?"

Lon's heart pounded. His blood felt as if it were boiling inside him. "No," he answered, his gaze never leaving her face. What if she knew more than she was admitting? What if, just what if, she were more involved than she was letting on? What if she'd been part of Alvare's trap?

"But Clive was involved with Federico?"

"What the hell did you come here for, Sophie?" Lon couldn't help the sharp note that had crept into his voice.

She better not be part of this.

God help her…God help him.

He was suddenly scared for her, scared that she was seriously in over her head, scared that maybe, just maybe, she'd gotten herself involved in Valdez' world.

"You're not one of them, are you?" he persisted, his voice curt, edged with violence. Even if she had gotten involved with Alvare and Valdez, there was no way in hell he'd give her up. No way in hell he'd walk away from her even if she'd turned…but she couldn't have turned. She couldn't have gone the way Clive did.

Sophie stared at him in shock. Her fine dark eyebrows arched with confusion. "One of who?"

"Them. The bad guys."

She laughed with disbelief. "Who are the bad guys, Lon? The way I see it, I've got two bad guys after me. Federico, and you."

"I'm not a bad guy."

She didn't say anything and he drew a quick breath, his mind racing. "If I were the bad guy," he added softly, watching her face, "you wouldn't have called me. You knew I'd protect you. You knew I wouldn't let anyone hurt you."

Sophie swallowed the lump forming in her throat. It was one thing to act cool, casual, indifferent—but it wasn't how she felt on the inside. She was terrified. She had a violent druglord after them. A husband with a shady past and Lon…Lon. Just who was he?

"I didn't set you up," she said wearily. "I'd never do that to you." Then she thought of how easily Federico had used her, manipulated her, to draw out Alonso. "At least, never intentionally."

Lon sat down slowly, settling in a spot a couple feet away from her. He winced as he reached for his food and a trickle of bright red ran down his bicep, beneath the cuff of his rolled up shirt.

Appetite gone, Sophie gave up trying to open her pouches. "You're still bleeding."

He shrugged and took a bite from his protein bar. "I'm not going to die."

"That's not funny."

He took another bite. "Not trying to be."

He was giving her one hellish headache. She stood and

wiped her hands on the back of her pants. "Let me have a look at your arm."

"You're actually going to touch me?" he mocked.

"Knock it off." She answered, kneeling beside him. She inhaled sharply as she peeled his sleeve higher to look at the wound. "There's a lot of blood."

"You never could handle the sight of blood."

There was amusement in his deep voice, a wry masculine amusement that made her feel foolish and feminine. "Knock it off," she said briskly, trying to find an impersonal tone when she felt intensely aware of him at that moment. Maybe it was because he was looking at her, his eyes riveted on her face and then her breasts. Maybe it was the size of his body and the ripple of muscle as he shifted his weight. "You'll need to take your shirt off."

"Careful, darling. Now you're exciting me."

She was tempted to punch him in the arm, right where he was wounded. "You're never going to change, are you?"

"You don't really want me to change."

She blew a strand of loose hair from her eyes. "Just take it off. You've lost too much blood."

"How do you know?"

"Even *I* have some common sense." She made a face, dropped her voice. "Just because I don't use it very often doesn't mean it doesn't exist."

"Interesting."

"Not really." She gulped in air. He'd begun to unbutton his khaki shirt, button by button and halfway through his shirt fell open, exposing the deep muscular planes of his chest and the flat, toned abdomen with its ripple after ripple of muscle covered by golden skin. He was in *amazing* shape.

Tantalizing shape. With abs like that a woman wanted to…

"All the way off," she said tautly, trying to focus her attention.

"It's stuck," he said, and he was right. The shirt fell off his shoulders but the fabric clung to the dried blood on his shoulder and upper arm.

Fighting her gag reflex Sophie carefully lifted the fabric from the wound, working it away, back and forth, until the shirt came away. But fresh blood immediately spurted.

"How are we going to stop it from bleeding?" she asked, trying to sound efficient, when in truth she'd begun to shake on the inside. She might have been in danger before, but she was in trouble now. Lon was trouble.

Big, big trouble.

"A pressure dressing," Lon said. He nodded at the pack. "I've got a small medical kit there, in the side pocket."

She found the small kit and opened it. "Stack two or three of the gauze pads together," he directed.

"Wait," she interrupted. "Let me use one of these alcohol wipes first." Her hands trembled as she ripped open one of the little packets. "And now, your arm. I want to wipe it as clean as possible."

She opened another packet and gently, gingerly cleaned as much of the wound as possible. She knew it hurt. He was very tense, but he didn't flinch when she dabbed at the wound. "I think that's a bit better."

"Now press the gauze where it's bleeding," he instructed flatly. "You want to press firmly. If we can stop the bleeding for about thirty minutes, we'll be all right."

"And if we don't?"

"We'll try a tourniquet." He smiled a little. "But not to worry, I think once we bind this up nice and snug, it's going to be fine."

She wasn't so sure. She hadn't seen this much blood since…since…*ever.*

Sophie wrapped the gauze tightly around his arm. It took a while. His bicep was big, the muscle rock hard. "What about the bullet?"

"I think it went straight through. Either that, or it lodged in the vest somewhere."

He'd taken a bullet. For her. Her eyes closed.

This was her fault. Lon had warned her about Federico. He'd told her Federico was more dangerous than anything she could imagine...

"I'm sorry," she whispered, concentrating on taping the gauze to his arm. Lightly she rubbed the edges of the tape, making sure the tape stuck to his skin. And facing him now, bandaging his arm, she realized she'd spent the past ten years running away from him. Running away from everything she couldn't control.

Because she couldn't control Lon.

Despite the strong attraction that had always existed between them, she'd feared his unpredictability. His instability. And what she'd wanted back then, and what she wanted even now, was stability.

A house, family, children, sisters, brothers, cousins. The whole thing.

"I'm *really* sorry," she whispered, and she knew there were many things she was apologizing for, many injuries and insults accumulated over the years.

Her eyes burned and she focused very hard on the white bandage on his arm. She could just make out a hint of red beneath the layers of gauze. The bleeding hadn't yet stopped. "I'm sorry for not telling you why I was meeting with Federico. I'm sorry for tricking you and flying out after the party. I'm sorry for dragging you into this mess."

He said nothing and she drew a deep shuddering breath, knowing that everything was changing, that whatever it was between her and Lon was growing stronger. More potent. More *dangerous*.

"Federico called you Alonso Galván," she added, her voice deep, hoarse. "Why?"

"It's an old family name."

"I told him you were Huntsman."

"Thanks."

She noticed he didn't elaborate. "Why does Federico know you?"

"Clive and I used to spend a lot of time together."

She searched his eyes, the blue irises cut with silver flecks. "How do they know Clive?"

"Clive made some…deals…in South America."

"With the Bank of England?"

"On his own."

This was the stuff she'd come here to discover. Lon knew what Clive had been involved in. Lon knew and yet he'd never told her. But before she could ask another question he pointed to the silver pouches still unopened in her lap. "You need to eat. You need to finish the sports drink. It's important you keep your energy up. We're not out of the woods yet."

He was telling her without using specific words that he wasn't going to answer any more questions, that whatever he knew about Clive's activities, he wasn't prepared to share.

She couldn't accept that. "I want to know. He was *my* husband—"

"And my best friend," he interrupted tersely, "but there isn't a hell of a lot I can say until we're out of here."

"Why?"

"Because it's complicated, and messy, and quite frankly, I don't have the energy to deal with what happened two years ago when we're in hot water now."

Okay. Good point. Sophie nodded a little. "Maybe this isn't the time to hash it all out, but when we're back to civilization you owe me the truth."

He just looked at her for a long unsmiling moment. "Eat."

Later, as Lon rearranged the contents of the pack, Sophie walked to the edge of the clearing where light poured through the dense foliage. The sound of roaring water grew even louder, to the point it was almost deafening.

Sophie felt a misting of water, and she drank in a breath. The fine spray cooled her skin, but her thoughts remained heated. Clive had been making deals in Brazil. Lon knew about the deals. Was he part of them? And what kind of deals were they? Then she remembered yesterday when she'd been interrogated, and they'd asked her about drugs...

About smuggling drugs...

Cocaine.

Sophie stiffened. Clive and Lon couldn't have done something like that. It didn't make sense. Neither of them had ever had anything to do with drugs. Why would they get involved with something so dangerous? Lon didn't need the money...but Clive did.

No. Clive wouldn't smuggle drugs. No way. No how. That was absolutely ludicrous.

But he had made quite a few secretive trips abroad...

"It's nicer near the water," Lon said, his voice coming from behind her shoulder.

She startled. She hadn't heard him approach. The noise of the falls drowned out nearly everything else.

She turned to look at Alonso. She tried to see past his icy blue eyes, his high pronounced cheekbones, his black hair brushing the collar of his shirt. She tried to see the man underneath and yet all she came up with was the teenage boy.

The angry rebel. The seventeen year old who'd been determined to never conform.

"How did you make your money?" she asked, thinking he'd never been wealthy, the McKenna-Huntsman family hadn't anything to their name. "It'd take a fortune to buy an emerald mine in the first place."

His eyes narrowed imperceptibly. "I'd been left some money from my biological father, and then there was a sizable settlement when my stepfather was hurt in the mine. My mother, stepfather and I bought one of the partners out."

"And eventually you owned the mine yourselves."

"Yes."

"So your family gave you a headstart?" she persisted, thinking he looked tough. Uncompromising. She couldn't believe Lon would be involved in something shady.

"I also had my own savings, Sophie. I'd been an officer in the Royal Air Force. I had a career. I invested carefully." He was studying her expression closely. "Why?"

"I don't know. I'm just trying to put it all together. Figure it out."

"Figure what out, Sophie?"

"You. This. All of this," she said gesturing to include the trees, the sky, the roar of the falls. "Nothing is making sense. I don't know you. I don't know why Federico would want you. I don't know how you found me so quickly, unless…" Her voice faded as she took a breath, trying to reconcile the Alonso that specialized in emeralds and international trade to the Alonso who'd stormed the camp in the early hours of the morning in a successful rescue.

Lon slid the pack over his shoulders, flinching a little as the straps rubbed across his injury. "I thought we'd decided we've leave this alone until we got home safe."

"I just want to know how you reached me so quickly. How you found me so quickly—"

"I have a surveillance team," he interrupted flatly. "And they have high-tech equipment."

"What kind of high-tech equipment?" Is this how he'd located Clive in Central America during the hostage crisis three years ago?

"Infra-red, GPS, sonar tracking devices."

The words *tracking device* unnerved her. "And when you say surveillance team…?"

"Friends."

Friends that sounded expensive. But none of them had spoken a word during the rescue and from their cohesive action, she knew her rescue wasn't their first. She felt a glimmer of possibility. "Was Clive ever part of your team?"

"No."

Of course not. The hope was dashed. The guys sneaking into the camp this morning had been pros. Lon had been a pro. "But this is how you got Clive out of Central America, wasn't it?"

"More or less."

She wasn't going to let him off the hook that easily. "And this…this commando…thing you do, it's not just a hobby, is it?"

He looked at her for a long moment. "Yeah, Sophie, it is. Some men go bowling. Some men play tennis. I personally like dressing up in army fatigues and playing Rescue Hero with a submachine gun."

"You have a submachine gun?"

"Come on, Soph, give me a break. I did what I did because you were in trouble. I don't enjoy this kind of thing. I don't feel more powerful carrying a gun. If I had my way I'd be in Rio soaking up the sun, enjoying a cold drink, not facing a night on a riverbank teeming with boa constrictors and alligators."

"Oh."

"Oh," he echoed bitterly. "You really don't know who I am, do you? You think I'm different than you. You think I'm cold, hard, without real emotions—"

"That's not it—"

"Well I don't enjoy roaming the world, living out of a suitcase, working night and day," he continued over her protest, not giving her a chance to finish. "I'm thirty-two. I'd love to settle down, have a couple of kids, take them to the zoo, the park, push my kids on the swing like any other dad." He stopped abruptly, ground his teeth together and shook his head. "But for some reason you don't see me as a just a regular man. In your eyes, I'm a machine. Something that performs on cue—"

"No, that's not how I see you. If anything I see all your emotions, I feel all your emotions and they're so strong they scare me to death. You, a cold machine? *Not a chance.* Machines are steady, practical, conventional. Machines run on automation. You're not a machine. You're the most intense human being I've ever met!"

CHAPTER SEVEN

"So you noticed," he grunted, his jaw jutted, eyes glittering. He was really mad now.

"Yes, I noticed. I noticed that just a little of something was never enough for you. You always wanted more. You wanted *everything*."

"So what's wrong with everything?"

"Because it's not…practical."

"Practical?"

"All right. Realistic. You don't get *everything* out of life. You get *some* things—"

"Bullshit. You limited yourself early on. You were afraid of wanting too much and being disappointed so you narrowed your options to one—Clive—disappointing yourself before life could do it to you, and simultaneously ensuring there'd be no surprises left."

"That is the single most arrogant, pompous, conceited, self-serving statement I've heard in my life."

"But it's true. And let me give you one more. A long time ago you got afraid, so you did your favorite Sophie trick: you played ostrich and buried your head in the sand. And that's how you've been living for nearly ten years, with your butt in the air, that pretty little head in the sand, without a clue as to why you're lonely and empty and unhappy—"

"I'm *not* unhappy." She was fuming. *Fuming*. So upset she could barely see straight.

"Okay, whatever you say, love, but don't complain when life's left you behind."

"I won't. And it hasn't."

He laughed. Damn his stinking hide. He laughed and he just kept on laughing.

His laughter goaded her beyond belief. Bending down, she grabbed a broken tree branch and brandished it like a weapon. "Stop laughing or I'll...I'll—"

"Do what, you cowardly little ostrich?"

Cowardly little ostrich?

Her jaw dropped, eyes bulged wide. In all her years she'd never been called anything so...so...humiliatingly puny. *Cowardly little ostrich?*

He was going to pay for that.

Sophie lunged furiously forward, shoved the stick between his ribs getting in one good jab before Lon caught the stick, immobilizing her.

"First lesson in survival, Johnson—"

"It's Wilkins!"

"Is never overestimate your strength." And with a swift yank, he pulled the stick from her hands. "One," he chanted, even as he swung the stick behind her legs, hitting the back of her ankles on her boots, knocking her feet out from beneath her. "Two."

Sophie landed backward on her butt. "Hey!"

Lon took another aggressive step forward, planting the stick on her sternum between her breasts. "Three."

Panting, she struggled to catch her breath. "Move the damn stick."

"Life left you behind a long time ago, Sophie Johnson. If it hadn't, you wouldn't be in Brazil two years after your husband died trying to figure out what the hell happened in his life."

"It's because I care—"

"Bullshit. It's because you're clueless. You never loved him. You *liked* him. You married him so you could keep playing ostrich and avoid a real life with me."

Alonso lifted the stick and tossed it aside. "Let's go. My point's been made."

He'd really enjoyed that little display of power, hadn't he? She grunted, feeling more than a little stiff and achy as she pushed off the ground.

Following behind him she plucked at the leaves and sticks and—disgusting!—big fat caterpillar in her hair. Sophie swiftly unbraided her hair, combed it out with her fingers and then pulled it into a softer, looser ponytail.

Cowardly little ostrich.

Each repetition made her angrier. Well, she'd show him, she seethed, following his rigid back downhill for nearly an hour. One way or another, she'd prove he was wrong.

They zigzagged down the slope, picking their way through the densest scrub imaginable, but Sophie's thoughts raced. He could call her a coward, but he'd run from his share of problems, too. For example. His family. As a teenager he'd virtually turned on his mother, refusing to have anything to do with her after she married Boyd McKenna. Lon had never bothered to bond with his step-father, much less have a civil conversation. Mr. McKenna had shown up for all the father activities at Langley and did Lon ever make him feel wanted? Did Lon ever go out of his way to show that he appreciated his stepfather's efforts?

No.

Sophie suddenly stumbled over a root growing out of the ground and sprawled into the brush.

Lon turned around, backtracked, returning to pull her to her feet. "Trying to bury your head in the sand again, darling?"

Unable to think of a single scathing response, Sophie brushed the leaves and dirt from her hands and glared at him with all her might. If only one of the boa constrictors he'd so casually—and unfortunately—mentioned awhile ago would drop from the canopy of trees and do a little constricting about his neck.

"Won't happen," he said, amused.

"What?"

He picked a last stray leaf from her hair. "The wishing-something-terrible-would-happen curse you're trying to put on me." He dropped the leaf and his lips curved in a cocky little smile. "It's already happened. You just don't know it yet."

"So you're going to drop dead later, when I won't be around to celebrate?"

His eyes glimmered. "I'm not going to die."

"Damn. And I was so hoping you'd leave me as your beneficiary."

"Sure. Marry me. I'll make you my beneficiary."

"Marry you? Never. I'd rather stay in the rain forest."

His eyebrows arched. "Not a bad idea. Not a bad idea at all." He turned and started walking.

She ran to catch up with him, puffing a little with the heat and humidity. As she reached his side a brilliant blue butterfly flitted past Lon's pack.

"You don't scare me, Alonso. I know you. You wouldn't leave me here alone. You wouldn't do it, no matter how mad you are. You're tough. Not cruel."

He looked down at her. His lips curved. It looked more like a snarl than a smile. "Who said anything about leaving you *behind?* Of course I'd stay with you. You and me, *carida.* We can play Tarzan in the forest."

"Ha ha."

"We *are* getting married."

This wasn't so funny anymore. Sophie stopped walking. "We're not getting married," she shouted at his big obstinate back.

"I'm glad you like the rain forest," he answered and he just kept walking.

Late in the afternoon they reached the river, with miles of land stretching out in a flat vista, the riverbanks bordered with palms and trees, Lon set to work.

He gathered wood. He whittled. He sawed with his knife. Lon, eyes narrowed, jaw jutted, attacked his tasks with palpable vigor.

His industry made her nervous. He was acting as if they were laying the foundation for their first home.

She watched as he stripped a long branch, and then carried the branch to two slender trees, tying it between the trees waist-high. Then it hit her. He was building a lean-to.

"Is this really necessary?" she asked, and the moment the words popped out, she wished she'd just bitten her tongue.

"It is if you don't want to become dinner," he retorted, bracing branches of about equal height against the long pole and lacing vines in and out, creating a loose mat, which he soon covered with dried palm fronds.

He was pretty resourceful, she admitted, and after a moment she began gathering more palm fronds and carried them to him. "Here." She set them at his feet. "And you're doing a good job," she added awkwardly.

A hammock materialized from Lon's pack and he strung it up between the two trees, beneath the shelter's roof.

"How long are we going to be here?" she asked, feeling the nervousness return. She and Lon out here, alone together. Dependent solely on each other. Somehow this didn't seem much safer than being held hostage by Federico and his men.

"A couple of days," Lon answered.

"And then?"

"Hopefully our boat comes."

"And if it doesn't?"

"We'll be here longer."

Caustic man. She swallowed. "And who is coming for us?"

"My friends."

"Same friends who were involved in this morning's rescue?"

"The same." He crouched by the river and rinsed off his hands. When he looked up she was standing there, next to him, hands on her hips, her eyes narrowed and focused on the horizon.

She looked too damn cute, he thought, fighting a smile. Sophie had always been such a…lady…but he loved her in her army green T-shirt, dark olive green pants and black combat boots. Her silky hair hung in a loose ponytail halfway down her back and her pale cheeks were sunburned. She could have been Barbie dressed up in G.I. Joe's clothes. God, he wanted her. Craved her. Couldn't imagine life without her.

He'd known ever since they were teenagers that they belonged together and Sophie, chicken that she was, wanted the easier emotion, the one requiring less courage, less confidence, less…passion.

But it wasn't really what she wanted. She was just afraid of wanting more, and of letting herself admit she needed more, and discovering she couldn't get it.

But in this case, she could. If she gave them a chance, she'd discover with him she could have a hell of a lot more.

But getting her to admit she wanted more, now that was the challenge.

She touched him lightly on the shoulder. "I think this has to be the most beautiful place on earth," she said quietly, breaking the silence. "I've always loved South America, but this…this must be paradise."

He heard the yearning in her voice. She wanted the beautiful places, she wanted the beautiful emotions back in her life. He didn't blame her. It'd been a long ten years for all of them.

"Did Clive ever visit Iguazu?" she asked, glancing down at him.

He shook his head. "I don't think so."

"He would have liked it here, wouldn't he?" Sophie saw Lon nod and standing there, listening to the river and the distant roar of the falls, she felt the strangest emotions wash over her. Wave after wave of hunger, sorrow, impatience, regret. When they'd all first met, there'd been so much potential…so much hope.

"We didn't have a good marriage," she said after a moment, swallowing around the lump in her throat. "But I'm sure you know that. He probably told you—"

"Never."

She chewed on the inside of her cheek, taking this in. "We struggled together. We…" she took a slow breath, finding this hard, harder than she expected, "didn't really fit, not the way we should have. I think Clive and I always got along because you were there. You were the part of us that worked. But once we'd married, you disappeared and Clive and I couldn't seem to even carry a conversation. He seemed so unhappy, Lon. He seemed so…lost." *And I was lost, too.*

Lon stayed silent and Sophie felt as if all the pressures of the world were on her head, bearing down, threatening to crush her. "Remember at Melrose Court, how you said I'd made my share of mistakes? You were right. I shouldn't have ever married Clive. I regretted it immediately. I regretted saying yes within an hour after he proposed. And I've regretted my decision every hour of every day since…''

She bit her lip, stared down at her feet, her eyes welling with tears. ''I should have ended it. Should have broken it off before we married but I loved Clive's father, and I didn't want to disappoint him.''

''And you didn't want to be free, because then you'd have to deal with me.''

A tear trembled on her eyelashes. ''I didn't realize what marriage was all about. I didn't realize what the rest of my life would be like.''

· She glanced down at the top of Lon's head, his black hair burnished by the sun, and she longed to touch his thick hair, longed to run her fingers through the weight of it against his neck. Instead she curled her fingers into her palm, fighting the flood of need. Oh, to be young again, to love again, to have the chance to make good decisions the first time out.

Her heart ached with emptiness. She'd messed up so badly. She'd done everything wrong and what killed her was she'd been so sure she was doing the right thing. ''I don't think I ever thanked you for coming to the funeral,'' she said after a moment. ''I never told you, but I was really glad you came. I couldn't have gotten through it without you.''

He stood up. ''I wouldn't not come.''

''Yes, but you flew in for the service from Santiago or Buenos Aires, or wherever you were, and except for greeting me at the church, we never had a chance to speak again.''

His forehead furrowed. ''We didn't speak after the service?''

''You don't remember?''

''It was a difficult day.''

True. The Countess was weeping wildly. Hundreds of

mourners attended the service. There was a slew of press and photographers hovering, and Alonso had arrived at the Cathedral extremely pale and withdrawn.

Now when she thought of that day, she felt sad, not grief stricken. "He tried hard to be good to me."

"He could have been better."

"You could say that about everyone—"

"No, I'm saying that about Clive." His mouth flattened. "You deserved better. You deserved more."

She felt her stomach knot. "He didn't want to die. He was young. He had big dreams."

"And those big dreams were more important than you."

"You can't live your life through another person. Clive loved me, but he had things to do. He had goals—"

"Listen to yourself!" He reached for her, hands settling on her shoulders. "Do you really believe this shit you tell yourself? Do you really believe that Clive chasing off all over the world was more valuable than the time the two of you spent together?"

She felt as if he'd punched in her chest. There was no way she could answer his question.

"I'll tell you what I think," he said, giving her a gentle shake. "If I had you, I wouldn't leave you behind for anything. I'd cherish every minute I had with you. If you were my woman I'd know what your dreams were and I'd care about your feelings, and I'd care about your needs, and I'd damn well make sure that you were happy. Loved. Satisfied."

Sophie closed her eyes.

"If you were my woman," he continued roughly, "I wouldn't send you to bed without kissing you, without loving you. I wouldn't go to work without letting you know that you are the most important thing in my life and that without you, my life would be empty. Without you, my life would be nothing.''

She couldn't hold the tears back. They were so hot. They seeped beneath her eyelashes. ''You can't say that—''

''I can. I've felt this way from the day we first met. You were so beautiful, and so goddamn smart. You had no idea how smart you were, or funny. You'd been all over the world, you'd been your father's traveling companion and every time he took a new job, he put you in a new school and from the sound of it, you handled it like a pro.''

''I hated it,'' she said opening her eyes and sniffing to keep fresh tears from falling.

''But you did it. You made your dad's life so easy. You made Clive's life so easy. They left you all behind and you took care of yourself. You kept yourself busy and you tried to be cheerful and sweet and it killed me then, and it kills me now. Why didn't you ever demand more? How could you not know you were worth more?''

His hand reached beneath the weight of her hair to encircle her nape, his fingers curving against the base of her skull. ''Ask for more, Sophie.'' His voice dropped, his fingers gently stroking. ''Want more. Demand more. You don't get more if you don't insist on it.''

''Tell me you want more.'' His thumb caressed her neck, a light tantalizing sweep across her heated skin. ''Tell me you're worth more.''

''My mother thought she was worth more,'' she whispered, ''and look what it did to our family—she divorced my father, ended up with a brand new husband and family—''

''You're not your mother.''

She looked up at Alonso. His eyes were hot, intent, smoldering with emotion that she'd never seen in any other man's eyes. Alonso wasn't like other men, though. He was fiercer. Stronger. More focused. "You don't know that."

"I know you."

She knew how much he cared for her. It was the depth of caring which terrified her. Her father had adored her mother—and her mother had crushed him. She couldn't be a goddess on a pedestal for Alonso. She wasn't goddess material. She was so ordinary.

"You think I don't know you," he said, sitting up, his voice so deep and husky it slipped like warm syrup through her skin, into her veins. "You think I'm just a fool when it comes to you." His mouth curved, a smile without a smile. "But I do know you, and I know why I love you. I love that you laugh at yourself. I love that you care so deeply for those around you. I love that you give people second chances, and third chances. Even me."

"No."

"Yes. You're giving me a chance right now." He suddenly grinned and Sophie's heart caught in her throat. She'd forgotten how damn devastating an Alonso Huntsman smile could be. He was beautiful when he wanted to be.

Unforgettable, too.

"No. I can't. I'm afraid of you."

"How can you be afraid of me?" he asked, voice deepening. "I'm supposed to be one of your best friends." His features softened, and his expression far away, as if remembering the way they'd been back in Bogota.

She felt some of her anger melt, remembering, too. She'd had the hardest time at Elmshurst. She'd made so many moves in so many years and by the time she reached Elmshurst she was thirteen and sick of being the new girl. One year at Elmshurst and she was still the new girl, still the odd one out.

Then she met Clive and Alonso at the fall mixer with Langley Prep, Bogota's elite boys academy. Clive had said something droll about the fantastic decorations—droopy blue and yellow paper streamers taped to the wall and a couple saggy balloons here and there—and Sophie had laughed.

"I say, be proud. The Langley colors and everything. You girls went all out," Clive added, and Sophie laughed again.

She'd never heard anyone deliver a line like Clive did. Clive was smart, funny, acerbic and it was such a relief after all the stuffy boarding school rules.

She was still laughing when Alonso turned and looked at her, and she felt his blue eyes pierce straight through her.

He hadn't said anything, he let Clive keep talking, and yet the corner of his lips lifted ever so faintly and she had the strangest impression that he found her intriguing.

From that moment on, Clive and Lon made her feel like one of them—smart, funny, fearless.

"We were all supposed to remain friends," she said softly, no censure in her voice, just regret. "We were supposed to grow old as friends."

Sophie's eyes burned again and she turned away, not wanting Lon to see her crying again. She was starting to fall apart out here. Something about Lon and the heat…the big sky and all the gorgeous tropical beauty…

It was so hard! She still cared so much for Lon, still felt so much when near him, but there was the problem of Clive, the problem of loyalty…the problem of being true to someone even if things weren't perfect.

She rubbed her forehead wearily, overwhelmed by everything. Was Louisa's Christmas party only two days ago? Had she only been in Brazil a day and a half?

"You're tired," Lon said. "You need to eat something,

and get some sleep.'' His sympathetic voice did nothing to help the lump filling her throat.

''You haven't slept, either,'' she answered, blinking back weary tears. What was it with Lon anyway? Why had there never been any resolution between them?

His expression was kind. ''Yes, but I'm used to going without sleep.'' He headed for the pack which he'd strung up in one of the trees, fished around inside and pulled out more foil pouches. ''Have a seat in the hammock, eat something, then get some rest.'' He patted the bedroll on the ground next to him. ''Rest. I'll keep watch.''

She was too tired to argue, and after eating another of the protein bars and packaged cookies he'd given her, she stretched out in the hammock, aware of Lon's big powerful body seated near her.

He was so strong. No one was as strong as Lon. Physically. Mentally. Emotionally.

Superman, she whispered, looking down at him, seeing how his black, rather shaggy hair framed his face. ''You're not in trouble with the government, because you used to work for the government, didn't you?'' she asked sleepily.

His brows pulled. ''Who told you that?''

''Clive.''

Clive, Lon thought. Of course.

Lon watched Sophie sleep. Clive, you bastard. What have you done to us? Sophie's not the only one who can't forget you.

Lon still didn't know how he'd keep Sophie from learning the truth about Clive. The easiest thing would be to confront her with the facts. He had proof in his office in Buenos Aires. He could show her Clive's downward spiral—the business decisions that crushed him, the financial need that buried him, the sellout to Valdez which cursed him—but the facts would shatter Sophie.

Hell, the facts had shattered him.

He understood why Sophie wanted to continue to believe in Clive.

She'd loved Clive. She loved the Clive she knew as a teenager, and Lon understood, more than anyone, the pain of losing someone so integral to your life.

Sophie wasn't the only one to love Clive. Clive had been the brother he'd never had. Clive had offered him unconditional love, the kind of acceptance he hadn't found even within his own family.

Sighing, Lon dragged a hand through his hair. God, there were times he still missed Clive. He'd never had a friend like Clive before. He doubted he'd ever have a friend like him again.

There were times all Lon wanted was to hear Clive's laugh once more. Clive had the best laugh…an honest-to-goodness belly laugh. It wasn't what you expected from an Earl's son. It wasn't a laugh you thought could come from a blond haired, blue-eyed polo playing fifteen year old, but Clive defied description. Clive defied everyone.

Lon smiled faintly. Maybe that's what forged such a tight bond between them. Both he and Clive were rebels at heart. Both wanted to define life for himself.

Clive had never wanted to go into the family business—banking was for bores, Clive used to say, and Lon's smiled stretched—but in the end, Clive did go to work for the Bank of England and he'd done well, at least, in the beginning. But Clive had been restless with the routine work, the lack of risk, the regular hours. He wanted to be in control of his own destiny. He wanted, ultimately, to work for himself.

And God help him, Clive invested in all the wrong things. At the time, the dot coms and start-ups had seemed like such promising ventures but when the market started falling, Clive lost everything he'd invested—and more.

The more is what drove him to destruction. The more hadn't been his to lose. The more—Melrose Court, his mother's savings, his father's life insurance—pushed Clive over the edge.

He could accept poverty for Sophie and himself, but how could he ever tell his mother, the proud Countess, that he'd lost everything she owned?

So Clive made a deal with Valdez. Clive, with his impeccable family connections, handled government and institutional accounts. Clive knew when money was being transferred to special government accounts in Latin America, and he knew when individuals would collect money from the various Latin America branches. For three million pounds, Clive gave Valdez the names and location of bank branches that government undercover officers visited.

One million pounds for each U.K. agent.

Lon was one of those MI6 agents.

CHAPTER EIGHT

Sophie woke some time in the night and the only light was the white glow cast by the moon. She stretched and turned to look for Lon. As promised, he was sitting next to her, keeping watch.

The hammock gently swayed as she turned on her side. "What time is it?"

"Almost four-thirty."

Sophie rubbed her eyes. She'd really slept. A good six, seven hours straight. "You must be exhausted."

"I'm fine."

He'd never complain, she thought, feeling strangely protective of him. She'd had it tough at Elmshurst, but he'd had it worse at Langley.

The headboy and prefects dogged Alonso. They knew Lon's mother had been single when Lon was born. They knew Mr. McKenna was just a surrogate dad. They'd taunted Lon and he'd never said a word, just escaped into sports. Into his music.

No one played drums like Lon. He could have been a professional drummer if he'd wanted. Instead he went to university and then the Royal Air Force.

"Do you ever play the drums anymore?" she asked, sitting up. "I'll never forget the time you played for me when I visited Langley. You loved that drum set."

"And the headmaster took them away not even a week later."

"But you played everything else anyway." She folded the blanket up. "You played everything you could get your hands on. It used to make Clive crazy."

"He was just jealous he didn't have a musical bone in his body."

"He *was* jealous of you," she said matter of factly. She slid from the hammock, and kneeling next to him, lifted the sleeve of his shirt. The top layer of gauze was white. She felt a wave of relief. It hadn't bled through. "But you know that. He hated how you made everything look so easy."

"Easy?"

"Yes. Easy. You're too damn smart for your own good."

Lon's eyebrows arched and he watched her unroll his sleeve again, covering the dressing. "Nothing came easy to me. I had to work my butt off. And I was always in trouble. Every school prefect, every headboy, every headmaster—"

"That's because you're strong. Your personality. Your values. Your outlook on life." She ran a hand through her hair. "You scare people, Lon."

He grinned. He looked downright proud.

"This is what irritates people," she added, wagging her finger. "You like playing the bad buy."

"It's fun." He shrugged. "And it helps that I don't trust people very well."

"Well, maybe you're going to have to trust me. I'm on watch now." She tossed the folded blanket at him. "You're going to get some sleep."

He grunted. "You think I'm going to trust you after what you've pulled this week?"

He had a good point there. But really, what could she do now? Where would she even go? "I've no tricks up my sleeve."

"Huh." But he was smiling a little and he settled into the hammock. "Maybe I should make you get in here with me—"

"That's really not necessary."

He laughed softly. "Cowardly little ostrich."

"Won't work. I'm immune to that taunt now." She took his spot in the sand beneath the shelter and wrapped her arms around her knees, studying him. He had such hard, masculine features. His eyebrows were a little too thick. His jaw a little too wide. His expression a little too brooding.

He wasn't classically handsome. There was no way one could call him classically handsome—not with a face that looked as if it'd been whittled from stone and then given a hard beating for good measure.

"Sophie?"

Alonso's husky voice wrapped viselike around her heart and she closed her eyes, held her breath, knowing, knowing in the deepest part of her that he'd always wanted her.

"You're supposed to be sleeping," she said hoarsely.

"I'm not sleepy."

She shook her head, denying him, silencing him, afraid of what he'd say next. "We can't do this," she whispered, suddenly too hot, her skin pulled too tight, her body strangely heavy. "This will never ever work, Lon. This has never ever worked."

Quiet greeted her feverish stream of words and she twisted her hands together, finger to knuckle, thumb to thumb, feeling each little bone and indentation.

Slowly Sophie looked up and Lon was waiting. Watching. She didn't think she could meet his dark eyes, couldn't face what might be there. Nothing Lon ever felt was light or teasing. His emotions ran deep. His intensity terrified her. He would move mountains to reach the one he loved.

He'd tear the world apart in search of his missing half. *She* was his missing half.

Sophie felt his gaze, felt the dark feral intensity within him calling to her, demanding her. She hunched her shoulders, turning her head away, refusing.

Still he waited.

She knew he'd wait forever this time. Now there was no Clive. There was no one standing in the way.

Her wide eyes found Alonso's and his gaze held her, intent, intense, sensual.

Clive had been but a temporary obstacle—a blip in the road—and Alonso, patient man, had been biding his time.

Waiting.

Resolute, determined, implacable.

Waiting.

Nearly seventeen years, waiting for her.

Hot emotion filled her. "What do you want?"

And still he said nothing, his blue eyes just looking at her, his powerful body relaxed. He appeared as if he had all the time in the world, and perhaps in a way, he did. Finally.

Her heart pounded even harder. Her mouth went dry. Sophie clenched her hands. *"Say something."*

A small muscle in his cheek pulled. He shook his head once, eyes growing darker, and she could have sworn she saw amusement in his eyes. Amusement and danger.

What an impossible combination.

It didn't help that he was making her feel the most impossible emotions. "Lon—"

He reached out, caught her chin in his hand, tipping her face up. His touch was so warm, he made her so hot and his fingers were like tongues of fire against her skin.

"What answer do you want this time, *carida?*"

She flinched and tried to pull away. "Don't call me that."

He didn't let her go. "But you are."

"No. You can't have me."

He smiled and yet she felt his energy, his body muscular, all leashed power and tension. "I've always had you."

Her blood pressure soared. Her heart raced. He should be locked up. Permanently. "You've never had me. You've never had any of me. Not my heart, not my body—"

"I've had a little of your body—"

"It was a kiss."

"It was more."

"It was a *kiss*."

"It doesn't matter." His eyes glinted, and he pulled her toward him, settling her on his lap in the hammock, her bottom—although covered by sturdy trousers—felt shockingly sensitive on his very warm, very hard lap.

His hand touched her face, two splayed fingers framing her mouth. "I know the truth," he added slowly, with husky emphasis, "and so do you."

Sophie felt caught, exposed, both female and sexual. Even her mouth took on a life of its own, lush and ripe and ready for him.

The truth? She thought wildly. The truth was that once upon a time Lon could hit a ball further than anyone else, figure out a math problem faster than anyone else, and made her laugh quicker, longer, but he'd also made her think too much and feel too much…like…*now*.

The frank hunger in Lon's eyes was making her mouth feel swollen, blood pooling in her lower lip, pulsing through her upper lip, heightening sensation in her until she felt all energy there in her face, in his hands.

He widened his fingers against her mouth, a slow caress that made her lips burn hotter, that stole her breath.

She felt as if he were opening her, taking her, and he'd only touched her mouth with two fingers.

But then with Lon she felt so much anyway, she felt so much tension and emotion, fear and excitement, hunger, frustration, resentment, adrenaline. He wasn't like anyone else.

He wasn't like her father.

Wasn't like Clive.

Lon made her feel like the center of a volcano, hot, hot, hot and far too powerful for her own good.

"You better stop," she choked, her heart which was beating fast a moment ago, now beating too slowly, her pulse dizzyingly thick, heavy, her entire body molten.

Lava, she thought. He makes me feel like lava and it's dangerous.

He's dangerous.

He wouldn't want to just make love, she thought frantically, he'd want to possess me in every way. He'd put his mouth everywhere and he'd take his time. He'd take an infinite amount of time and he'd make sure I loved it, too. He'd turn me inside out, make my body come alive, make me feel everything and then I'd lose all control. I'd never be able to keep all the feelings within me.

His head dropped, his lips brushed hers, brushed his own fingers still framing her throbbing lips. "What's the worst that could happen?" he whispered against her mouth. "If I did to you what I want to do to you, what you need me to do to you, what would happen?"

I'd like it too much, she silently answered, her bones melting as his lips brushed her mouth yet again, setting her on fire on the inside, a thousand dragonflies shimmering, wings glowing red and gold. She was feverish. She was beside herself.

If Lon kept kissing her mouth she'd want him to kiss her neck, the hollow between her breasts, her tight aching nipples. She'd dig her hands into his thick glossy black hair and hold him to her and beg him to devour her.

Make me feel like the volcano again.

Make me burn. Make me melt.

Make me come.

I don't really live. I just exist. I barely know myself anymore.

But he still knew her, and he still—despite all—wanted her. He still saw the youth in her, the fire, the fierce American girl she'd been.

He remembered her laughter, remembered her intelligence. And he wanted her. *To simply be wanted* was the biggest turn-on of them all. Physically. Emotionally.

Lon's fingers parted her mouth wider, and she saw his own lips curve in a small smile when he covered her lower lip with his, she let out a strangled cry.

It felt like heaven.

Lon's kiss turned her inside out.

No one, she thought breathlessly, as he lifted his head what seemed like hours later, *no one,* had ever kissed her that way.

Granted, she'd only kissed Clive, but when Lon kissed her, it wasn't like a kiss, the way one thought of a kiss, lip to lip, mouth against mouth. It was like breathing. Like feeling. Like being completely alive for the very first time.

"The truth," he repeated, running his thumb across her trembling mouth. "Remember. The truth. It's all we have, Sophie."

The truth…

Sophie stumbled to her feet, took several steps away, legs weak, body traitorously warm, everything on the inside hot and shivery.

He wasn't supposed to make her feel this way. He'd had this effect on her at Elmshurst. He'd made her feel so raw, so physical, so…*hungry.*

She felt Lon's gaze follow her as she dropped to her knees in the sand, no strength in her bones.

"Everything okay?" he asked, stretching his arms behind his head.

He was smiling. He was loving every minute of her agony. Sophie dug her nails into her palms. "Go to sleep."

She kept vigil for the rest of the night, and in the dark the muted roar of the falls was a kind of music, coloring the rain forest's immensity.

She did want more. Sophie flexed her fingers, pressed on her knees. She'd wanted more as long as she could remember. And the wanting more scared her.

But maybe more didn't have to be bad. Maybe more wasn't selfish, or vindictive. Maybe more could be getting out from under her mother-in-law's shadow, starting a career...

Maybe more could be going into the foreign service like her father. She would have loved to be a diplomat. An attaché. She spoke four languages, three actually tolerably well—German, Spanish, French—and she understood a little Russian from her early years with her father in Moscow.

What a life she'd once lived. She hadn't appreciated it when she was younger, had hated all the traveling and boarding schools, the tutors and weeks of intensive foreign language instruction. Submersion, they'd called it, placing her and her father in an environment where English was no longer spoken and everything became the new language, every thought and need expressed in the new language. The first two weeks of each submersion program nearly drove Sophie mad but now she saw that she'd been given a gift.

Sophie watched the sun rise over the thick horizon of green and the roar of the falls sounded louder, fiercer. Something dormant in her stirred to life. Not many American girls had been able to see what she'd seen...do what she'd done. There was no reason for the adventure to be over. No reason at all.

Lon woke a couple hours after dawn. Sophie knew the moment he awoke. The quiet morning suddenly felt charged, tension returning but she was determined to keep her distance, not wanting a repeat of last night's kiss.

He'd done something to her body with that kiss, she thought sitting off by herself, in the shade of a tree not far from the river's edge. He'd made her throb and ache and crave for hours after he'd gone to sleep.

She tried to focus on the butterflies flying thick around them, yellow and white, brilliant blue, spotted greens, but she couldn't ignore the weight of Lon's gaze. She knew he was watching her, knew he was curiously amused by her attempt at distance.

Well, let him be amused. She would *not* be seduced by Lon. Or by desire.

The air grew thicker and Sophie's mood grew worse. She was hot. And hungry. And she needed to get away from Lon.

How could a day last this long? How could she wake up and do this whole dreadful waiting thing again tomorrow?

She needed rain. A hard tropical downpour to cut the humidity, never mind the terrible pressure building relentlessly within her. She belonged in cool quiet places, not this muggy inferno that felt as physical and raw as Alonso himself.

Wait, was that a breeze? Eagerly she lifted her face up, tugging at the neckline of her shirt. The hint of moving air tantalized her and yet when she opened her eyes the palm fronds were still. No leaves stirred on the trees.

Lon wandered leisurely toward her, hands in the pockets of his trousers. "You look miserable, love."

She grit her teeth together. "I'm *hot*." *And you're not helping, Huntsman*.

He smiled. He knew. He knew exactly what he did to her. Yet he feigned ignorance. "Cumulonimbus clouds," he said. "Thunderstorm's heading our way. That's why the pressure's building."

"Great."

"It'll cool off once the storm hits. But that's still a couple of hours away. Depends on the wind."

"What wind?" she demanded, looking up, and too late she realized this was just what he was waiting for.

He *wanted* her to look at him. Wanted her to see the flicker of heat in his eyes, and feel the hint of his fire.

That fire had been in the kiss last night. It was there every time he looked at her.

"Don't," she whispered, taking a hasty step backward. "Don't do that again."

"Do what?" he asked with mock innocence.

"You know." She felt her cheeks heat, her skin tingling at the memory. "You kiss too good."

She'd never thought she could handle Lon, or the intensity that was him, and yet when he kissed her in the hammock with his hard body covering hers, it'd felt *right*.

The heat and warmth and intensity had been perfect, and his kiss, his touch, had been more real to her than anything she'd ever known.

His kiss was muscle and fire, heat, sinew, bone, blood strength.

It made her reckless, fearless. It made her want the world.

He couldn't hide his smile. "Don't sound so stricken, Sophie. Good kisses aren't supposed to be bad things."

Says who? she wondered, staring rather obsessively at his mouth, studying the way his full lips curved, the upper lip slightly bowed. What an amazing mouth. What a beautiful shape. Why hadn't she ever noticed his mouth before? It was his mouth which gave his face warmth... kindness. His eyes were cool, the scar on his cheekbone stark, but he had a generous mouth and when he kissed...oh, he had to be the most generous man in the world.

What she'd realized in the hammock, with Lon's arms around her, his hard chest pressed to hers, was that she really wanted a man to want her.

She wanted a man to need her.

She wanted a man to strip off her clothes and make love to her and then promise to do it again and again until she was seventy and wrinkled and gray.

Hot tears burned and itched the back of her eyes. She felt a lump swell in her throat. Everything was starting to go haywire on her, and it was all because of Lon.

"You're going to change everything," she said.

"I intend to."

"And you liked kissing me."

His eyes gleamed. "Yes."

"You're not the least bit apologetic."

"Not at all. I'm glad I kissed you. I'd like to kiss you again." His lips curved in a secret smile, and she felt his amusement. "In fact," he added after the smallest hesitation, "I think I will."

He reached for her, drew her toward him with the assurance of a man who knew exactly what he was doing.

Lon slid his hands around her neck, his thumbs stroked the hollow in her throat and she inhaled sharply, his touch making her skin feel hot and tight.

His head slowly descended, covering her mouth, throwing her straight back into sensation. It was a light kiss, a teasing playful kiss, and yet it created wave after wave of pleasure within her. Her tummy tightened. Her lower back prickled. She felt heat flood through her middle.

It was just a kiss, she told herself. But God help her, it felt like so much more.

Lon lifted his head, brushed her sensitive mouth with the pad of his thumb. His lips, those amazing lips that left her weak and breathless, curved. "Even better the second time," he said with evident satisfaction.

She swayed on her feet, staring at the middle of his green shirt. Yes, she thought, rather dazed. It was better the second time.

"Want to go cool off somewhere?" he asked.

She kept her gaze fixed firmly on that invisible point on his thickly muscled chest. "Please."

She didn't have to look to know he smiled. "Follow me."

She did, but she felt as if she was walking in a fog, and she was certain he knew his kiss had knocked her senseless again.

This is his payback, she thought, scrambling downhill and despite Lon telling her not to grab at plants to steady herself, she couldn't help throwing out her hand now and then to stop herself from falling.

His kisses were his way of torturing her. His idea of revenge was slowly, deliberately turning her on, stoking the flames, and letting the heat build until she was crazy with need.

And then what? She wondered, as Lon never did anything by chance. What would happen once he'd pushed her self-control over the edge?

Nearly an hour after leaving their camp, they reached the bottom of the dark rocky incline, and Sophie could hear water roaring. She took a step and realized she was stepping into air. Lon grabbed her by the back of her pants and pulled her towards him.

"Keep your back against the rock, and follow close after me." He slid his pack off. "We're going to enter a cave up here. The mouth of the cave is pretty low. It'll be a squeeze getting through but once we're on the other side, we'll be all right.''

She just nodded. Her heart was still pounding. She hadn't liked the feel of air beneath her shoe. Nor had she liked how her nerve endings went nuts when his hand brushed her backside. Lon was tying her in knots.

Getting down on her hands and knees, she followed him through the cavern opening. He hadn't been kidding about the tight squeeze, either. They crawled through the cave on their stomachs, wriggling like inchworms and yet Lon, twice her size, managed to get through the tight space in half the time she did. No man should be in such fantastic condition.

As she finished her belly-crawl, it seemed as if the sound of water was everywhere…dripping from the top of the cave. Running in steady streams down one side of the inky wall. Roaring in torrents just outside the cave.

Leaving the passage, she got to her knees and Lon helped her the rest of the way up. ''Look.''

Sophie stared in wonder. They'd entered a circular sheltered cove. It was like being in the middle of their very own tropical paradise.

Before them water fell in tiers like that of a wedding cake, layer after layer of foamy white water and the mist rose in iridescent clouds.

Water cascaded everywhere. Verdant ferns and mossy plants blanketed sheer rock cliffs. Massive black rocks protected a circular shaped pool of the clearest water imaginable.

They were in the middle of the falls. ''This is—'' she swallowed, shook her head, overwhelmed ''—breathtaking.''

His gaze met hers and Sophie saw heat in his eyes, a flare of hunger that he either couldn't—or wouldn't—

hide. And the desire she saw there made her belly knot, her mouth dry as dizzying heat flooded her limbs.

The knots inside her grew tighter. Harder. She felt as if she'd do anything to escape the tension.

"If you're still hot, the water's safe to swim in here," he added, voice husky, rasping across her senses. "Or you can rinse off under that cascade."

Yes, cool off, she thought, touching the tip of her tongue to her upper lip. Good idea. She did feel hot. Unbearably hot. Not humid hot, but sultry hot, hot on the inside, hot underneath her skin where her pulse pounded and desire balled in her belly.

She dragged herself beneath the cascade, showered in her clothes before stripping off the wet trousers and T-shirt and showering again in the gentle waterfall in just her bra and panties. The water was cold, but the steady pressure on her back, shoulders and scalp felt wonderful and it did cool her off, ease some of that incredible fire simmering beneath her skin.

Calmer, Sophie found a big flat rock and lay facedown on a smooth expanse, letting the sun warm her skin and dry her hair.

From her vantage point she could see Lon start to climb from the pool. She turned her head, closed her eyes, telling herself she didn't want to see that.

Or did she?

Sophie groaned into the crook of her arm. It was getting really hard to keep a firm grasp on reality here. Reality— London, Louisa, Melrose Court—seemed like another world away.

Reality was swiftly becoming Lon. And wanting Lon. And craving more of Lon.

Reality was going to kill her.

Lifting her head, she watched him wade from the pool, nearly naked and dripping wet. His white briefs showed more than they concealed and she glanced at the size of him, the shape of him, and felt the air catch in the back of her throat.

Sex with Clive had been…okay. Sex with Lon would be…? How would it be?

Fantastic.

No, she corrected, you can't make assumptions like that. Just because he kisses like that, doesn't mean he'd be all that good in bed. Of course, it *could* be good, she thought, trying not to shiver as he walked toward her, his big body golden everywhere, his skin flawless, gleaming, droplets of water shimmering like diamonds on his gold skin.

Her mouth dried. Her heart pounded. But sex could be really, really bad, she mentally added.

What if he was too aggressive? What if he took her so hard and fast it hurt?

Or, worse, what if he had no staying power?

Or maybe he wasn't really big. She'd heard really muscular men sometimes had little…parts…not that his looked so little just now.

Alonso stood over her. "Feeling better?" he asked, head bent, water dripping from his black hair down his neck, onto his chest and lower.

She licked her lips. They were so dry. She'd never remembered them this dry before. "Yes," she croaked.

"Good." He lifted a hand, ran it through his wet hair, scraping it back from his face. His bicep bunched. His tricep rippled. His abdomen tightened.

She tried not to stare at the sleek tanned abdominal muscles disappearing beneath the waistband of his briefs. She felt the strangest urge to trace the muscles in his stomach, curious to feel the texture of his taut golden skin. He looked so healthy, so primal, so male. "Thank you."

"So, have you thought anymore about my proposal?"

"What proposal?"

"Marrying me."

She nearly choked on her own tongue. "That wasn't a proposal, Alonso, and you're out of your mind if you think I'd even seriously consider it."

"Why?"

"Because I'm...."

"Widowed?"

Sophie's face burned all over. "*No.* You're not right for me. I'm not right for you. And I don't feel that way about you."

He crossed his arms over his chest. "Now that's a lie, Sophie, and you know it," he said pleasantly.

She scrambled into a sitting position, suddenly wishing she had her trousers and T-shirt back on. "It's not a lie. We have—a certain spark, yes—and maybe once upon a time I had feelings for you, but...marriage? Come on, Lon, get real! I'll never marry again, and I'd certainly never agree to a bogus marriage with you!"

CHAPTER NINE

HER passionate outburst was met by silence.

And he'd thought she'd become so coolly unemotional, Alonso mocked, staring down at her, watching her sunburned cheeks turn dusty-rose, her blue eyes deepen with flecks of violet and navy.

Oh, was he wrong.

Lon's gaze dropped to her mouth. There was nothing cool or unemotional about Sophie. Her bare lips were full, the upper lip beautifully dark pink, almost red. He'd loved the kiss last night. Loved it even more this afternoon even though it'd been brief. But in that brief kiss, he'd felt her shudder against him, her body going soft, pliant, and he knew she'd be more than eager and willing in his bed.

And maybe she didn't love him, but she wanted him. And she was a very curious girl.

He felt his lower lip curve, his body hardening as he remembered the way she checked him out as he climbed from the pool.

He saw the craving in her eyes, felt the hunger in her lips, in the softness of her mouth. Felt the desire when she trembled every time he touched her.

She might say she'd never marry again, much less a *bogus* marriage to him, but there'd be nothing bogus, or loveless about their relationship. It'd be very real, very hot, and very satisfying.

Lon crouched down in front of her. Sophie's eyes widened. She tried to scoot backward but he wasn't about to let her escape. He caught her bare ankle in his hand and held her captive before him.

But Sophie wasn't giving in without a fight. She flung her hands out, grabbed for any crevice in the rock she could cling to.

Her puny little fingers were no match for Alonso's strength and he pulled on her ankle a little, keeping her firmly in front of him.

"Define bogus," he said, kneeling on either side of her ankles, hands on either side of her knees.

"Fake!" she tossed at him, cheeks dark with color.

He bit the inside of his cheek to keep from smiling. "You think this is fake?" he asked, lightly strumming his thumb across her warm, flushed cheek.

The ice princess was no more.

Sophie was practically panting, her breasts, barely contained by her little lace bra, rising and falling with short, shallow breaths. "I don't know what you mean."

"No idea?" he mocked, leaning forward and kissing the side of her neck.

She gasped. She stopped wiggling.

He kissed her a little lower on her neck and she sucked in a rough breath. "No idea?" he repeated softly, lips curving in a slow, wicked smile. "You feel nothing?"

She nervously touched her tongue to her lip. "Well, not exactly nothing."

"What then?"

"Hot."

Desire shot through him, sharp and hard. "Let's see if I can cool you down." He leaned near her, covered her mouth with his.

She tasted like wintergreen, cool clean wintergreen but as he parted her lips with his, her coolness turned to heat. He flicked his tongue across her upper lip and then the inside of her cheek, kissing her slowly, taking his time as he explored her warm soft mouth.

Sophie whimpered as he deepened the kiss and her

hands moved to his chest. He wore no shirt and her fingers pressed into his skin as if somehow trying to hold him, grip him.

He urged her back, pressing her onto the sun-warmed rock, first her shoulders, then her ribs, and last her hips. When she was completely stretched out he moved above her, bare skin brushing bare skin. She shivered as his body grazed hers, and he hardened yet again, hardening all over.

He wanted to possess her, wanted to know her, but wanting even more for her to recognize her desire first.

Lon parted her lips with his, teasing her, giving kisses that weren't deep or satisfying and her hands slid up his chest, and down again in a mindless search for satisfaction.

She was no ice princess, he thought. She was hot, really hot, and her softness, her warmth, her hoarse pleading was pushing him over the edge. He sucked the tip of her tongue, drawing it into his mouth, loving the feel of her, loving the taste of her. She shivered and shuddered against him, almost helpless now in his arms.

Sophie clung to Lon, her head spinning, nerves screaming. Her body had taken on a life of its own and her muscles shivered, shuddered, rippled. She couldn't lie still, couldn't keep from arching up against Lon, trying to get closer, trying to become part of him.

She'd never felt so wanton. This was what she'd always wanted to feel, and she couldn't get enough.

He lifted his head a little and she strained against Lon, straining to close the distance, and her hips moved of their own accord.

Lon placed a hand against her throat, fingers spanning her jaw, and he opened her mouth wider to him. He was letting her know how it'd feel being open to him, how it'd feel being open beneath him.

She made a soft, hoarse sound in the back of her throat. Hot, she thought, she was so hot all over.

Lon slid a hand between her legs, caressed her thighs and parted them for him, making room for him between her thighs.

Yes, she thought, hips, belly, body nearly dancing, trying to reestablish contact. *Take me. Fill me. Make me part of you.*

She gasped as she felt him settle between her thighs, felt him rock forward ever so slightly, his erection pressing against her warmth and dampness. She felt her dampness. She knew she was as turned on as she could possibly get. He'd lit her completely on fire.

Covering her lips with his, he thrust his hips into her, and she felt the hard length of him push between her thighs, pressing into her softness, against all the electrified nerve endings in her body.

She arched against him, wanting to take him, wanting all of him and not getting it was maddening. She dug her nails into his chest, ground her hips up, and sucked his tongue hard, as if to say, do this, do this to me.

But he didn't and she felt as if she was going to pop out of her skin. Sophie had never been so hot and sensitive and the friction of his hard body made her desperate to have his hands on her, desperate to have her body explored.

If only she could feel him free of his briefs and she slipped a hand from his chest to his waist, her fingers pulling at the waistband of the briefs. She wanted to touch him, cup him. She wanted to guide him into her.

Just as her fingers stroked his shaft, he rolled away from her and stood up. "Feel cooler?" he asked, running quick fingers through his dark hair.

Sophie couldn't catch her breath. She lay on the rock, dazed, pulse racing, heart pounding. It felt like molten lava flowed through her veins.

"No," she answered shortly, slowly sitting up.

"That's interesting," he said, bending down to meet her gaze. "Because if this were bogus—*fake*—you'd be cool by now. You'd be colder than cool, you'd be ice. People who don't like each other, people who aren't attracted to each other, can't get this turned on."

"That's not true," she panted. "Lots of people can get turned on by sex."

"Yes, *carida,* but what I was giving you, wasn't sex. It was me. It was me loving you." He stood up and his expression was curiously hard, detached. "So, if you want me, and I think you do, then you're going to get me. Along with a ring, a marriage license and the promise of the rest of our lives together."

She was shaking head to toe, her skin, body, heart on fire. She felt so much at that moment she couldn't even put a coherent thought together. "You don't have to get married to make love."

"Really?"

She wrapped her arms around her knees. "Make fun of me. I don't care. I'm not ashamed to say I just want some great sex. I've never had that, but I have had a husband."

"Was he a great husband?"

"Shut up."

He stared down at her, considering her. "Ironically, Sophie, I've had lots of sex, including lots of great sex, but I've never had a wife. Not even a lousy wife. I'd love a wife."

"Mr. Clever, aren't you?" she flashed, getting to her feet. She knew his gaze brushed her breasts, her hips, her bare legs, but she wasn't going to act all virginal now.

She'd been with a man. She knew about body parts. She had some. He had some. So there.

She forced herself to walk as normally as possible to the place she'd left her clothes to dry in the sunshine. And despite her shaking hands, she tried to dress normally, too, zipping the dark green pants and tugging the T-shirt over her head.

Once her boots were back on and snugly laced she met him by the grotto entrance.

He knew she was a mess. He knew she couldn't manage these kinds of emotions. Or this kind of tension.

You're not going to get rid of him this time, Sophie, she whispered to herself. But she didn't really want to get rid of him, she just wanted him on her terms.

She wanted an easy, *comfortable* relationship. She glanced up into his hard features. And marriage to Lon didn't match her definition of easy *or* comfortable.

"What part scares you?" he asked, and his voice practically hummed through her, prickling her skin.

It was uncanny how well he could read her. She pulled the hair elastic from the pocket of her pants and looped her hair into an easy ponytail. "All of it."

"Nice and specific."

She let the elastic snap. "Okay, I'll give you one. Trust. I don't trust you."

She felt the way his eyes narrowed as he stalked toward her, his shirt rolled high on his biceps. "Have I ever let you down? Have I ever failed you? Tell me one time when I deserved—"

"You haven't told me the truth about Clive."

Lon stopped walking. He stood in front of her, tall, immovable, and silent.

"Or the truth about you and these crazy rescues you do with your *friends*. Or how you and Clive became involved with Federico."

Still Lon said nothing.

Sophie shoved her hands into her pockets, trying to control the crazy emotions somersaulting through her. "You've never told me the things I have to know—"

"And those things will determine the way you, what...*feel* about me?" His voice was cutting. His sarcasm made her flush. "Is this your way of sorting out your feelings? Learn about Clive...decide about Lon?"

"No."

"Because, *muñeca,* in case you didn't know, Clive and I are separate people."

"I know that."

He shot her a hard look, resentment seething in his blue eyes. "I don't think you do." He bent over, grabbed the pack from the ground. "Let's head back. The storm's moving in—"

"Stop walking away from me every time you don't like what I say!"

"I don't. But I'm not going to stand around and argue when we have a storm heading our way."

But they didn't get far before the dark clouds overhead opened and warm rain fell in hard drenching sheets. It was impossible to keep climbing the steep slope with the rain slashing down, and Lon tugged her hand, forcing her to join him beneath the relative protection of a big tree.

Rain pelted palm fronds and the broad glossy leaves of the tropical undergrowth and Sophie tried to stand stiffly apart. "I had no idea how much you hated him," she choked, wrapping her arms around her chest, trying to contain her hurt and shock, anger and sadness.

She couldn't bear it if Lon had turned on Clive, too. As it is she felt guilty for wanting out of her marriage, but she did love Clive, and she did want the best for him, and Lon and he had been friends before she'd ever met them...

Lon wrapped an arm around her and drew her closer so that she leaned against him. "I don't hate Clive. He was like my brother. At one point, I would have done anything for him."

"Yet you're so angry when you talk about him." She was shivering, not from cold, but from all the pent-up emotion circling wildly inside her.

He sighed, and lightly rubbed her back. "I don't want to attack him. He's not here to defend himself, but yes, I have a hard time with the way things ended. I have a hard time that he left you alone, that he left you broke, that he did all this after taking you from me."

"Lon, he didn't take me from you—"

"He knew I was going to propose." His hand stilled. "I'd seen the perfect ring, but I wanted Clive's opinion. He knew you, knew your tastes. He agreed you'd love it. I bought it."

She tensed, every muscle tightening in protest. "But you and I had never really dated, and we'd only had that one kiss."

He shrugged. "I didn't want to rush you. You were close to finishing your university studies and I wanted to give you time. I wanted to court you properly."

She heard the mockery in his voice. He was mocking himself. Mocking his good intentions. He'd wanted to woo her, behave like a gentleman, and instead he left the door open, let Clive walk in.

Sophie closed her eyes, pressed her face to Lon's chest.

"You don't know how I struggled, Sophie, when I heard that he'd proposed while I was out of the country. I couldn't believe he'd do that to me. Couldn't believe—" he broke off, mouth compressing. "It took me a long time to forgive him."

Her fingers tangled in his shirt. She struggled to find her voice. "I had no idea."

He made a rough, impatient sound. "I never meant to tell you." He wrapped her ponytail around his hand, tugged on it a little. "I shouldn't have said anything now. I'm not a very good loser."

"But the issue isn't you losing. The issue is us, being able to have a real conversation. If we're such good friends, if we're supposed to have…trust…then we should be able to talk openly, honestly, about everything." An emerald green lizard darted on a branch, daringly close to Lon's shoulder. "We should be able to talk about Clive. Us. Life. The *truth*."

The corner of his mouth lifted in a dry smile. He reached out and traced one of her dark eyebrows, following the high arch over her brow bone.

Sophie drew in a deep breath, his touch did something to her. Each time. Every time. She couldn't help her response. Even that light gentle caress along her brow sent sparks of fire everywhere. She wanted to lean against him, melt into him. She wanted more.

More and more and…

"Clive. Us. Life." He repeated her list back to her thoughtfully, his finger brushing the delicate skin just beneath the arching eyebrow. "That's a lot of truth."

"We can handle it, can't we?"

"*Can* we?"

"We have to be able to handle it," she answered, her voice husky.

His blue eyes warmed and he shook his head a little as he looked down at her. "You're so unbelievably beautiful."

She couldn't speak. She could only stare up into his face, wanting, wanting, wanting.

This is how she'd felt that very first night they met, at the Langley-Elmhurst Mixer. Clive, in his own masterly way, had shoved them together for a slow dance and Sophie had been terrified.

She'd never slow danced with anyone like Alonso Huntsman before. He didn't seem like a teenager. He was already built like a man. And that night, with his arms around her waist, his hands resting in the small of her back, she felt every shift of his hips against hers, felt the hard curve of his thighs.

He'd been so warm, and he'd held her with such confidence, and in the dark school gymnasium decorated with blue and yellow paper streamers and clusters of pale blue balloons, she felt fragile, delicate, small.

Lon's big body dwarfed hers. His big personality paled hers. His fierce drive intimidated her. But that didn't stop her from dreaming.

But that's how she'd always left it. Just a dream. Something far off and fantastic. Never reality.

Sophie realized the storm had passed. Rain still dripped through the trees, but the sun had broken through and the jungle now steamed. Birds squawked above the wet ping of water and the smell of the rich damp soil.

"The rain's stopped." Lon's voice rumbled in her ear and a shiver raced through her. "We better get back."

It was nearly dark when they reached their campsite, and in the twilight Sophie spotted a boat on the river, and two men hunkered down near what had once been their lean-to shelter. The lean-to branches were broken, the palm fronds scattered. Stunned, she moved close to Lon.

The men stood as they approached. Both were dressed casually, one wearing shorts, T-shirt, and a red baseball cap, the other shorts and a yellow windbreaker.

"Flip," Lon greeted the man in the red cap. "You're early."

"We need to move you out," Flip said evenly. "Things are getting exciting."

Lon didn't ask. Instead he tossed his pack to the second man and lifting Sophie, waded into the river and placed her in the back of the boat. "Put on the life jacket," he told her, climbing in next to her.

She did, and she sat down in one of the seats in the middle. Lon sat down next to Sophie, practically sprawling in his seat, his big body relaxed, but his eyes were intense.

The second man, the one in the yellow windbreaker, took a position across from Flip. The men weren't talking. They each looked very alert. Focused. Something was up, she thought and their alertness made her skin crawl.

What was going on? Had Federico figured out where they were? Had something else happened?

They motored slowly up the river, away from the falls. Night had fallen and except for the moonlight they traveled in darkness. The river was wide and silent and the only sign of civilization was the lights dotting the dark banks from the odd vacation home.

Sophie couldn't bear the suspense any longer. She leaned toward Lon, lowered her voice. "What did he mean by 'things are getting exciting'? And don't give me a brush-off. We're only doing the truth now."

Only the truth, Lon thought, gazing down into her pale face. She was terrified but she wanted the truth.

"Miguel Valdez, Federico's boss, has arrived."

"Federico has a boss?"

Her naiveté would have been funny if it weren't so dangerous. "Federico doesn't go buy milk without getting permission from Miguel Valdez."

Flip suddenly indicated for them to be quiet. They were nearing a massive steel bridge. They passed beneath a massive arched bridge and the stream of car headlamps shone like a white neon beam above. Then the bridge was behind them and all was dark again.

A few minutes later Flip guided the speedboat into a hidden quay, motor humming softly. From the thicket of trees surrounding the quay a light flashed once, twice.

"We're clear," Flip said, turning the engine off.

Lon climbed from the boat and assisted Sophie out. The men's silence, the forest's stillness, unsettled her. She reached for Lon's hand, holding it tightly as he set off, up the steep stone stairs leading to the big house.

"Where are we?" she whispered, passing through iron gates.

"A safe house."

She shot him a swift side glance. "So I've got my own bedroom, with a door that locks?"

He smiled faintly. "Not that kind of a safe house. You're protected here, but you're not safe from me."

It was a big lodge-style vacation house with a soaring beamed roof, gleaming yellow hardwood floors, and native Indian rugs scattered everywhere.

She did have her own room, right next to Lon's, and their rooms were connected by an adjoining door. She glanced at him. "And does that one lock, too?"

"No." His warm gaze met hers and held. "Have a problem with that?"

She shook her head.

"Good. Dinner's ready. Let's eat."

The Argentine dinner of grilled steaks and crisp, salty French fries waited for them, and it smelled wonderful, but Sophie found she could barely eat with Lon's hot, slumberous gaze following every bite she took, watching her mouth as if it were the most fascinating thing he'd ever seen.

"Don't make me take my dinner into the kitchen," she said, heart thudding, body lazy and weak.

"I'd just follow you in."

"Why?"

He laughed once, low, mocking. "Why do you think?" And his gaze dropped back to her mouth, his eyes practically caressing her lips, before looking back into her eyes with blatant naked hunger.

He looked so deeply into her that she felt as if he'd physically touched her, reaching into the middle of her with his hand, reaching inside where only he could go.

He wanted her. He wanted her more than anyone had ever wanted her and he was going to love her, all of her, with his eyes and his hands and his mouth and his body.

It was all there in his smoldering gaze, the things he wanted. The things he'd give.

Pleasure. Endless pleasure. But she had to trust him. She had to give herself to him. He'd have it no other way.

She trembled inwardly. Her skin grew flush, her breasts ached, tingling as her nipples hardened, tightening.

A mind kiss, she thought breathlessly, a mind kiss that didn't stop at the lips but slid down her neck, between her breasts, along her belly to the heat and damp between her thighs.

He would have her all.

She swallowed with difficulty. "You said…" she tried to swallow again, her voice high, faint. "You said…"

"I said?" he prompted, smiling, all masculine satisfaction.

"We'd wait. Until I agreed…until we…"

"Married." His smile deepened. The intense satisfaction glowed in his eyes. "So yes, we will wait."

He had to be bluffing. "You can't really mean that. It's absurd."

"Not to me."

"I don't *want* to be married."

"Shame. I have a hundred different ways I'd like to make love to you."

"You can't make love in a hundred different positions—"

"Did I say positions?" He lifted his wine goblet, the overhead light gleaming on his bent head, emphasizing the hard stark line of his cheekbone, before looking at her, his eyes flickering with a secret sensual fire. "I don't think I said anything about positions although there are many I think you'd like, and several I'm sure you've never tried."

The air caught in her throat. She stared at him, lightheaded, dizzy, curious beyond belief, seeing flashes of them naked together. His body above hers…his body beneath hers…his body behind hers…

She exhaled slowly, getting hotter by the moment.

There was no way he'd really wait until they were married. Lon had had sex a million times in his life and marriage had never been part of the equation. "You really won't do anything with me until…?"

"You're mine."

She pressed a shaking hand to her throat, tugging on the edge of her T-shirt, finding it hard to breathe. She needed air. Ice. The longest coldest damn shower ever. "That's hopelessly old-fashioned." She tugged on her T-shirt again. "You're not old-fashioned."

He drained his red wine and then pushed away from the table. "Says who?"

"Me. I know you." She glared up at him, seeing him, feeling him, wanting all that size and hard muscle stripped bare, pressed to her. "You would have made love to me in the back seat of the Wilkins' Bentley in Buenaventura if I'd let you, and I was only seventeen!"

His gaze dropped to her flushed chest, taking in the shape of her full breasts and the tight hard nipples which felt as if they were about to pop through the T-shirt. "You had great breasts even then. All I wanted to do that night was get your nipples in my mouth.''

She clenched her thighs together, denying the empty aching sensation between. He *was* torturing her. He was trying to force her into a marriage by withholding sex, and it blew her mind. No man withheld sex from a woman. That was a female trick. It was manipulative, cunning, sadistic...

''Your breasts were so soft. I don't think any woman has breasts as soft as yours,'' he continued. ''I was dying to suck those incredibly soft sweet nipples—''

Sophie noisily pushed her own chair back, knuckles shining white from fisting her hands so hard. ''Well, that's a lovely little story. Good night, Alonso.''

She saw a cool, controlled silvery light in his eyes. ''Good night, Sophie.''

And she felt his wretched victory smile follow her all the way down the hall.

CHAPTER TEN

NO DREAMS were more sexual, more physical, than the dreams Sophie dreamed that night. She woke nearly every half hour, hot and miserable, to look at the clock and pray for morning—and relief from these erotic dreams to end.

But each time she closed her eyes again, the dreams returned and he was so good in the dreams, so persuasive.

She felt his mouth on her all night.

She felt his eyes burn her as he explored her.

She felt his hard body pressed to her and yet each time she reached for him, he eluded her. And when she'd hunch away from him he'd kiss her back, her shoulder, her bare neck and she'd turn back over and return to him. Wanting his mouth. Wanting his eyes. Wanting his hard body and all that warm, sleek skin.

Bastard.

Sophie woke violently, hands gripping tangled white sheets, her body damp covered in perspiration.

She felt exhausted, absolutely wrung out, and yet her body throbbed relentlessly from her lips to the back of her knees, and every place in between begged for touch. Craving release.

He'd ruined her. Without even possessing her. Ruined her by *not* possessing her.

Had there ever been such a criminal mastermind?

She rolled over onto her stomach and buried her face in her pillow.

But this wasn't really about sex. She was calling it sex.

She was turning it into a physical thing in a pathetic attempt to protect her heart.

It was so ludicrous. *She* was so ludicrous. She'd married Clive to ensure that Lon couldn't—wouldn't break her heart.

Lon represented intense emotions.

Clive represented peace and stability.

And hadn't that whole thing been a joke? Clive was not stable, her marriage had not been peaceful, and as it turned out, Lon was the steady rock.

Lon was her rock.

Just like he'd always been.

Sophie felt tears burn her eyes and she bit her lip, and dragged the pillow up, around her ears as if she could just hide herself forever.

She'd screwed their lives up. She wasn't a cowardly little ostrich. She was a cowardly *humongous* ostrich. She'd made a decision that had hurt everyone—her, Clive, Lon—and here Lon was, giving her a second chance, and she was even hesitating?

She sat up, balled the pillow in her lap, held it to her stomach. She loved Lon. There had never been a time when she didn't love Lon. So he did scare her a little with his intensity, but he'd learned to temper it a bit in the past ten years. He was still passionate, but he laughed more now. He made jokes. He was far more patient. Much less argumentative.

And he wanted her.

He wanted a life with her, and she wanted everything he seemed so willing to share. His heart, his mind, his body, his life.

She wanted to share his life, too. She knew she'd enjoy a life with him…could imagine herself married to him. Could picture herself waking with him, having breakfast with him, teasing with him. It'd be like the holiday in Buenaventura but better because they were older and wiser, and definitely humbled by reality.

But there were obstacles. There were things Lon didn't know about her.

She could be a spendthrift. Harrod's would always remain her urban paradise.

She could be impulsive. Accepting Clive's marriage proposal had been a totally knee-jerk reaction when she heard that Lon had left the country again for another three months.

And she could be destructive. She would have divorced Clive if he hadn't died. There was no way she could have stayed in that marriage for the rest of her life. It was too empty, too lonely, too devoid of love.

Well, there it was. Not a pretty picture, but it was what it was. And she'd tell Lon the truth about her. Let him see her exactly for who and what she was. And if he could live with that, then yes, he could live with her.

Marry her.

Love her. Just the way she loved him.

Sophie reached for her robe. She'd go talk to him now.

She heard the shower running in his bathroom and she pulled her robe closer, thinking she'd just have to come back. Then the shower turned off and she froze.

Just do it, she told herself. Knock.

She did. Lon opened the door, his upper body naked and damp, a white towel wrapped around his hips.

"Morning," he said, grabbing another towel and rubbing his hair dry.

She watched the muscles rope and ripple all the way down his body. "Good morning."

Lon dropped the towel he'd been drying his hair with

onto his shoulder. Sophie's eyes were huge, and sorrowful. She looked like she was on the verge of tears.

"I have to talk to you," she said.

"Have a seat," he said, pointing to the wide marble lip surrounding the bathtub.

She perched on the black marble, rubbed her hands against her thighs. She opened her mouth. Closed it. Swallowed and tried again. Her mouth worked. Her eyes filled with tears. "I am an ostrich," she said painfully.

This was the serious matter she'd come to discuss with him? It was all he could do not to smile.

"And I have run from you, or more accurately, run from myself. Not because I don't care. But because I care so much." Her upper lip quivered and she fought to get control. "I loved you since…since our first slow dance together, but loving you is like loving a Greek demigod."

"Just a demigod?"

She ignored his jest. "You're not exactly mortal, like the rest of us. At least, you don't seem like the rest of us."

"Superman?"

"Sort of. I never felt like I belonged with you. I couldn't imagine a life with you." She glanced down, at the edge of her robe. "Maybe I didn't even try to imagine it."

He felt a terrible tenderness inside him. "And what part of this is supposed to surprise me?"

She swallowed, bunched her hands in her robe pockets. "I honestly believed I'd be happy without you. I honestly thought after I married Clive I'd forget you." Her eyes burned and she concentrated on her robe sash. "But I couldn't forget you. I couldn't stop thinking about you. I couldn't stop hating myself for not doing the right thing when I should have."

He moved toward her, and she jumped away, moving to the sink. "No. Let me finish."

His chest burned. She was punishing herself—and maybe once he wanted her to hurt for the pain she'd caused him—but that was long ago, and no longer part of who he was, or what he wanted. "You don't have to put yourself through this. I know you had regrets, Sophie. I knew you were unhappy at times. But I admired you for trying to make it work. I respected the fact that you didn't quit, that you didn't walk out—"

"But I did." She looked up at him, stricken, her reflection ghostly pale. "That's the horrible thing. I did want out. I wanted out so bad I couldn't stand it." Despite her best efforts, tears were falling. "I filed for divorce, Lon."

He stilled. "You did what?"

"I filed for divorce the day before Clive died." She'd begun to shiver and she couldn't seem to stop. "And no one knew…but Clive."

Lon stared at her for what felt like forever. Time seemed to stop. Change. Take on a life of its own.

"We talked the night before he died," she continued. "He was in Sao Paulo. He called me from the hotel. And he was upset. But he wouldn't tell me why. I was so tired of him not talking to me, so tired of his moods and secrets and—" She broke off, pressed a hand to her forehead, trying to calm herself. "I just blurted it out. I said, 'Clive, I'm done. I can't keep living like this.'"

Lon turned away, walked the length of the bathroom, stared at the blank wall. "What did he say?"

Sophie cried harder. "He said, 'Okay, darling. Whatever you want. Whatever you need.'"

Lon bunched his hand into a fist and he hit the wall.

He hit the wall again.

He heard Sophie sob behind him. *Hell, hell, bloody hell.* It was all beginning to come together. It was all starting to make sense. And it was worse than he ever imagined.

Clive had seen it all coming, hadn't he? There had been no swift end for him. No sudden darkness, no sweet bliss.

Sophie was still crying. "Please forgive me, Lon. Forgive me. He can't, so you must."

Her broken voice finally pierced the fog in his brain. He heard her teeth chatter and he turned. She was literally falling apart, huddled against his sink.

He stared at her for endless seconds, transported back in time to that one perfect school holiday they all spent together in Buenaventura.

Clive's father had made it possible. He'd somehow convinced the other parents that it'd be all right for the three teenagers to share their holiday together, assuring all that there'd be plenty of chaperones.

But of course, once they reached the Wilkins' extravagant summer beach house in Buenaventura, no one paid them the least bit attention, and for two weeks Clive, Lon and Sophie had done exactly as they pleased.

They'd stayed up half the night, slept until noon, stumbled to the beach and they'd all been so easy together. So deliriously happy.

But the two weeks came to an end and with their bags packed, the Wilkins' chauffeur loaded Sophie's small suitcase into the back of the limousine and Earl Wilkins tossed the boys suitcases into the trunk of the Bentley and it was time to say goodbye.

Clive handled it in typical fashion. Cheerful, optimistic, droll. But Sophie…beautiful Sophie with her long dark hair and lovely arching eyebrows shook her head. "I can't go back," she said, tears filling her eyes. "Don't make me go back. Please don't make me go back."

The Earl had glanced helplessly at the boys. No one knew quite what to do. Then Countess Wilkins took charge.

"Shame on you," Louisa cried, briskly descending the stone steps of the tall pale pink stucco beach house with the dark red terra-cotta tiles. "You're seventeen, Sophie Johnson, nearly an adult. Get in the car and stop this nonsense now."

And Sophie had gotten into the back of the car, but Lon had never forgotten her expression.

She looked absolutely, positively alone, and certain she'd be that way all her life.

"There's nothing to forgive," he said roughly, his voice harsh in the cool, sleek marble bathroom. "We are who we are—and exactly who we've always been."

She stared at him. "What does that mean?"

"Clive was gay," Lon admitted tersely, moving toward her, his eyes riveted to her swollen face, cheeks wet with tears.

"Gay?"

Lon's gut churned. His insides were on fire. He didn't want to hurt her, didn't want to hurt Clive, didn't want to hurt any of the good memories they had left. But she was in her own hell of guilt and grief, and it wasn't what Clive would have ever wanted.

"He loved you, Sophie." Lon hesitated, wondering, how much did one say? How much could one say? "He needed you, too. You were his...cover. You gave him what he thought he was supposed to have."

Sophie was shaking her head. She couldn't believe it, couldn't accept it. "He never said anything...he never did anything. He never looked at other men."

Lon swallowed. *Because he was in love with me.*

Yet Lon couldn't tell her, not because she wouldn't understand—Sophie, of all people would—but it was a secret Clive had kept his entire life. Clive had never acted on his feelings, and it was only in dying, did he confess that he'd loved Lon. That he'd married Sophie to keep Lon part of his life.

Lon had made a promise that night to protect Clive's memory for his family, and to protect Clive, too.

Clive had died a miserable death, and despite Clive's mistakes, despite his short-comings, he deserved love.

Standing before Sophie now, Lon felt the past and future fly at each other like two rockets on a collision course. "For the longest time I was angry with Clive. I felt he'd deserted you. I thought he'd died and left you with nothing. But now I see it's not true." His voice dropped, gentled. "He didn't leave you with nothing. He left you with me."

Sophie lifted her head and looked into eyes, her heart bruised, her thoughts scattered, swirling, hopelessly confused. "He should have told me," she whispered. "He should have talked to me. I would have at least understood—"

"He couldn't. He was proud, and he was a Wilkins. Once he'd committed himself to the idea of being a husband, and a family man, he couldn't bear to disappoint you, or his parents…or…me."

There was something in the way he said the last word, something in the *me,* that made her skin prickle and the air catch in her throat.

Or…me.

She looked into Lon's eyes and there was no calm there, no peace at all. Instead he burned internally, burning with pain and a rage that had nothing to do with their conversation and everything to do with the way they'd lived, and the way Clive had died.

Clive had been in love with Lon.

Clive had been in love with *Lon*. But of course. She closed her eyes, pressed the heel of her palm to her forehead. But of course he had.

She shook her head, opened her eyes. Her Clive…*their* Clive…had lived the most tortured life. Why had she not seen it before? "How long have you known he was gay?"

Lon's features tightened, twisted, in a mask of pain. "Not long before he died."

Wordlessly Sophie left the bathroom, returned to her bedroom and rummaged through the dresser looking for something to wear. She put on a long linen skirt and a cotton top and headed outside to the wide deck overlooking the river.

Clive. Her husband…her *friend*…forced to live such a secret life…

The sliding glass door to the deck opened, closed. Alonso appeared at her side. "You shouldn't be out here. It's dangerous."

She glanced at him briefly. "You're the one they want. Not me."

He was silent a moment, studying her. "Are you okay?"

"No."

"Do you want to talk?"

"No." And it was true. She couldn't talk right now. She'd come to Brazil to discover the truth about Clive's world but it wasn't the truth she thought she'd find. "I need some time."

"Fine. But come inside. I can't leave you out here."

She spent the rest of the day alone, curled up in the

middle of her bed reading a book the Texan named Flip gave her. It was a big paperback thriller, written by a popular American crime writer. Sophie tried to read it but tears kept filling her eyes.

No wonder they'd all been so unhappy. It was a love triangle, a wretched love triangle like no other.

The three of them, such misfits and outcasts in Bogota, had formed a powerful and unlikely friendship in their adolescence, and somehow they'd carried that friendship in adulthood.

Despite all. Despite everything. Despite their flaws and faults. Despite the hard things thrown in their way.

Sophie blinked, wiped away another tear that had spilled over yet again.

Poor Clive. Thinking of him struggling along, struggling so alone with such a secret burden, nearly broke her heart.

She'd loved him. She would have never married him if she hadn't cared about his happiness, but her love had never been romantic, just as his feelings for her had never been romantic.

She almost laughed as she cried all over the book in her hands.

They were such fools. No wonder she and Clive had stumbled into marriage together. He was an ostrich, too!

Sophie did laugh this time, and then she sobbed. She felt horrible beyond belief and she desperately wanted to apologize to Clive—*I'm sorry I wasn't a better friend to you*—and to Lon for never taking a chance when she should have.

Lon deserved so much better.

She'd believed in Clive's smiles, the Wilkins' lovely beach house, the Bentley, and of course, the Earl himself, who was good and decent and kind. But she hadn't believed enough in Lon. She hadn't believed he could provide the stability, or security she craved.

What a stupid girl she'd been.

Suddenly a hand touched the top of her hand, and she reached up for that hand, knowing it was Lon, knowing he'd come for her, knowing he'd been there for her all along. She held his hand tightly, terrified of letting him go.

His fingers tightened around hers. "It's been a hard day," Lon said quietly.

A lump filled her throat, and her eyes already raw from crying so much welled with fresh tears. "Very."

"He should be here tonight. If he were, we'd sit around playing a mean game of cards and we'd say all the things we should have said while he was alive. We'd tell him the things he needed to hear."

"Like?"

Still holding her hand, Lon sat down on the bed next to her. "That we'd always love him, whether he was gay or straight, and that we'd always be his friends, no matter his sexual orientation."

Sophie studied their hands, and the way their fingers twined together. "Stay with me tonight. No sex. No kissing. Just be here."

"I'd love to."

She fell asleep with his arms wrapped around her and she woke a couple times in the night, reaching out to check and make sure Lon was still there in bed with her. He was. Then she'd move closer toward him, and close her eyes once she'd made contact with him again.

Thank God for Alonso. She didn't know what she would have done without him. Not just this week. But always.

Waking the next morning Sophie found her face buried

against Lon's chest, and his arm wrapped snugly around her waist. It was the most warm, cozy feeling in the world.

Opening her eyes she met Lon's gaze. "Hello."

"Sleep all right?"

"Yes. But I had crazy dreams." She stretched a little, and felt his hand slide across her abdomen, filling her middle with heat.

"What did you dream about?"

"Us. All of us. Clive, you, me." She turned to look at him. "Yesterday was so surreal. Everything you told me…everything we've gone through. If we weren't real friends we wouldn't have survived this, would we?"

"No." He kissed the top of her head. "But we are real friends. Clive was our real friend."

She sighed. "So this is what you meant last week when you said Clive was complicated." She closed her eyes thinking of it all yet again. "And Louisa. There's no reason to tell her, is there?"

"No." Lon hesitated. "She's been through enough, and she might not understand."

Sophie pictured Louisa home alone at Melrose Court. The old Georgian house was enormous. Louisa must feel so alone right now. And it was almost Christmas, too. "I should call her, though. I feel badly that I left her right before the holidays." A lump filled her throat. "I feel badly that she's so alone period. No family, no grand-children, just her, her house, her title."

Lon tucked a long tendril of her hair behind her ear. "Phone her when we get to Argentina. Invite her out for the New Year. I can send my plane for her."

"We're going to stay in Argentina?"

"For a while." He studied her face. "I thought you could use some sun and rest. I've a house down in Mar del Plata, on the coast. If it's all right with you, I thought we could go there. Honeymoon there.''

She sat up and looked down at him.

"Or is there somewhere else you'd rather go for our honeymoon?'' he persisted.

The lump in her throat grew. ''You've said honeymoon twice now.''

"You're paying attention.''

She struggled to think of something coherent to say. He was proposing, wasn't he? ''I haven't been the most successful wife. Why would you want to marry me?''

He made a rough sound in the back of his throat and sat up to kiss her firmly. ''I love you.''

She stared into his light eyes. ''That's it?''

He kissed her again, more gently. ''Should there be more?''

The lump in her throat was making it hard to swallow and her eyes felt gritty, itchy. ''No, love's exactly the right reason.''

"Good answer,'' he said gently, tucking another strand of hair behind her opposite ear. ''So marry me. Today.''

"Today? How? Where?''

"Here.'' He grimaced. ''I've got a bored priest desperate to go home.''

"You have a priest here, right now?'' Alonso had taken the Boy Scout motto of being prepared to the extreme.

"When Flip and the boys airlifted supplies in a couple days ago, I asked them to bring along a priest. He didn't mind coming along for a day or two—I've offered to build them a new parish hall—but it's Christmas Eve tomorrow and he's anxious to get back to Posadas for Christmas services.''

Sophie felt as if she was on the roller coaster of her life. ''We're getting married today?''

"Today. Tonight." And Lon suddenly grinned, like a kid on Christmas morning who's just gotten the bright shiny red bike he's always dreamed of. "That way Father Perez can fly home."

She stared at him, thinking he was the most confident, most optimistic man she'd ever met in her life, and she was actually beginning to like it. "Did the priest happen to bring along a dress for me to wear?"

"Father Perez doesn't have much experience with ladies' wear. However, I made sure an appropriate dress made it onto the plane along with the clergy."

Lon thought of everything, didn't he?

They had breakfast a little later in the dining room, and then Lon met with Flip and Turk and she tried to finish the book Flip had loaned her, but her attention kept wandering off and she found herself shaking her head.

Married.

She was getting married. Today. To Lon.

Incredible.

Late in the afternoon she took a long bath, soaking in the tub and trying to relax in the ginger scented bubble bath, but her heart pounded like mad and she kept rising out of the tub to look at herself in the mirror.

Yes, that was her face. That was her hair all knotted up on top of her head. That was her chin wearing a white bubble beard.

She was getting married. To Lon. In just an hour now.

She sat down again and pulled the plug on the tub. She was getting married in an hour!

Drying off, she rubbed the ginger scented body lotion into her damp skin, and stepped into the slim sheer white lace dress Alonso had bought for her, trying not to think about later, trying not to think about what might be happening oh…two hours from now.

Three hours from now.

Four hours from now.

Seven hours from now.

Could they make love for seven hours? She paused, glanced again at her reflection, saw the tumultuous emotions in her face, but above all, saw the shine, the hope, the excitement.

Yes, seven hours of lovemaking was most doable.

The priest was old, very thin, and very nice. He was Jesuit, like the priests that had first come to Brazil and Argentina from Spain and Portugal two hundred years earlier. He greeted both Lon and Sophie with a fatherly kiss. They sat down together, the three of them, and the priest went over the ceremony before expounding on the theme of marriage itself.

When he concluded his thoughts on marriage, and marriage's unique state of grace, he asked if they had any questions. Lon and Sophie both shook their heads.

Father Perez smiled. ''Then now we will have the ceremony.''

The ceremony itself took less than fifteen minutes— less than Father's discourse on marriage—and Lon's friend, Flip, stood up as his best man, and the Argentine housekeeper stood with Sophie as her matron of honor. But as Father's words of blessing poured over them, Sophie felt a buzz of light and heat, and the strangest, strongest impression of Clive suddenly being there with them. And then it was gone and Sophie felt a wave of utter peace.

Her eyes stung but she didn't cry. She blinked and Lon suddenly reached out, brushed her cheek and she saw a welling of happiness—and tears—in his eyes.

Had he felt Clive's presence, too?

Then Father was saying the final, binding words, "And I now pronounce you man and wife."

Blinking tears, she lifted her face to Lon's and his lips covered hers in a searing kiss.

He loved her.

He loved her.

She suddenly caught his face in her hands, pressed a kiss to his mouth. "Thank you."

His hand wrapped around her wrist, holding her palm to his cheek.

"I love you," she added.

"I know."

"You do?"

"I've always known."

She wanted to disappear with him right then and there, but they had paperwork to do first. Funny, Sophie had never remembered this part with Clive, hadn't remembered sitting down to fill in and sign the marriage certificate. She watched and waited while Flip wrote his name as witness, and then the housekeeper.

Then the priest showed her where to sign. Sophie picked up the pen, ink pen poised and she read the certificate, written in Spanish.

Her name, Sophia Elizabeth Johnson.

His name, Alonso Tino Galván—

Galván.

Galván? How could it be? They'd talked about this. He'd said it was an old family name and yet here it was on the wedding certificate.

"No," she choked quietly, temper rising. She dropped the pen, stared at the certificate for another moment before pushing away from the table. She wasn't going to sign it. They'd agreed on the truth. They'd agreed to *only* the truth. But he still wasn't being honest with her, still wasn't telling her everything.

Would he ever?

Lon was moving toward her. ''What's wrong?''

She kept backing away, her fingers kneading her white lace skirt as anger rushed through her, making her head spin. ''Who the hell are you?''

CHAPTER ELEVEN

LON glanced at Flip and the priest, who discretely disappeared. Lon shut the door behind them. "You know who I am," he said, walking back toward her.

She wasn't going to fall for this again. He could act calm and reasonable, but honestly, how could he think this wasn't an issue? "I know Alonso Huntsman," she answered, feeling very unprotected in her thin white lace gown. "But I've never met Alonso Tino Galván, and that's who this piece of paper says I married. *Alonso Tino Galván.*"

"Sophie."

"Don't patronize me. You've been Alonso Huntsman since I met you."

"Huntsman's my mother's maiden name. Not my legal name—"

"Why did you use Huntsman then? You were enrolled in school as Huntsman."

"My mother wanted to protect me. She worried what others would say if they knew I was Tino's son. My father agreed with her. Thus I was raised Huntsman."

"What's on your birth certificate?"

"Galván."

Of course. She clenched her hands. "I *asked* you about Galván, back in the rain forest, and you said it was an old family name. You didn't say it was *yours!*"

"It's not a name I've ever really used."

"But the priest knows it. Federico Alvare knows it—"

"Galván became one of my aliases."

155

She was literally shaking with anger. She couldn't even think of a thing to say next. She knew the Galván name. The Galváns were as well known in Argentina as the Kennedys were known in the United States. The Galváns were wealthy. Powerful. Aristocratic. "We've been friends for years and years, and yet you've never mentioned the Galváns. Never told me anything about your father's family. And yet Tino Galván was your father, wasn't he?"

"Yes."

"Don't you think this was something you should have told me?"

"It didn't strike me as important. It's just a name."

It wasn't just a name. It was a family. *His* family. "Have you ever met any of them?"

"I met my brothers and sisters for the first time a couple years ago. I've never met my late father's wife."

"She's still alive?"

"His second wife, yes."

Sophie returned to the table, stared down at Lon's name. Alonso Tino Galván. Not just any Galván, but Alonso *Tino* Galván, named for the late Count Tino Galván. "What are they like? Your brothers and sisters?"

"They're good, smart, hardworking people."

She sat back down in the chair she'd left earlier. "Not the spoiled rich you read about?"

"No. They have money, but they're far from spoiled. They've had a great deal of heartbreak and troubles. That's actually how I met the first of my half brothers and sisters. Through my work here in Latin America." Lon took a seat opposite her at the table. "I discovered that someone was shopping a Galván baby around. The black market wasn't really my area, but the Galván name caught my interest. I had to look into it."

"And?"

"The child for sale was really a Galván. Only he wasn't a baby anymore, he was a young boy, and it took a year—a very frustrating year—but eventually Anabella and Lucio were reunited with their missing son."

"How long had it been since Anabella had seen him?"

"Not since his birth." Alonso's features hardened and he shook his head. "For five years the child bounced from foster home to orphanage to foster home. Foster families were afraid of adopting him, afraid of the Galván name." His mouth twisted. "It can be a terrifying name."

"You're not afraid of it."

He shrugged, lifted the certificate, studied the names printed on the page. "My mother loved my father deeply. Passionately. And I know he loved us, too. He set up a trust fund for me. He made arrangements for my mother to be taken care of after his death. He wasn't a perfect man by any means, but he was my father. I do feel a loyalty—if not for his sake, then for my mother's."

"Does Boyd know all this?"

Lon's face could have been carved from stone. He didn't move a muscle, didn't blink. "Boyd knows he'll never be my father, but he also knows that Mother needs him. She was devastated by Tino's death. If it weren't for Boyd, she wouldn't be here today."

"Just like if it weren't for you, I wouldn't be here today," she answered, reaching for the pen.

"But you love me." His hard jaw finally gentled. "Deeply. Passionately."

She leaned across the table, plucked the paper from his fingers, and kissed him. "Deeply," she repeated softly. "Passionately. Alonso Tino Galván."

It was true, she thought, a half hour later, wandering around the bedroom suite with the bottle of chilled champagne. She did love him deeply, passionately, but she'd never been more nervous in her entire life.

It's not like you're a virgin, she told herself, glancing at the cold bottle's gold and white label. You've had sex. You know the mechanics of it.

But oh, it seemed so different when she thought about sex with Lon.

The door opened and Lon appeared in low pajama pants that barely hugged his hipbones and an open robe which left the broad planes of his chest gleaming in the soft bedroom lighting.

"I'm still dressed," she said, ridiculously self-conscious all over again. "Should I have changed?"

"No." There was an edge in his eyes, an edge to his voice. He was looking at her as if she were the last woman on earth. "You haven't opened the champagne?"

"I was waiting for you."

"Thank you." He moved toward her, relieved her of the bottle and opened it easily. The cork popped with a bang, and smiling faintly as the champagne fizzed, Lon reached for a glass from the tray on the dresser and filled her one flute before handing it to her. "Drink."

She took a sip and handed the flute back to him. He drank deeply, and then wrapping an arm around her waist, brought her against his chest. Dipping his head, he kissed her, slowly, so slowly, that she felt her bones melt, her legs dissolving, her body folding into his.

"Dance with me," he whispered against the corner of her lips.

"There's no music."

He kissed her again, lightly, near her earlobes. "Yes, there is. If you close your eyes, you can hear it."

And he drew her even closer against him, his hands

sliding down the length of her spine, molding her to him, shaping her waist, her hips, the curve of her bottom. "Listen." He dropped kiss after kiss along the column of her throat.

She listened.

At first all she could hear was the wild fierce drumming of her heart, and the blood roaring loud in her ears, and then as he held her, her cheek nestled to his chest, she heard the deep steady beat of his heart.

It was such a strong steady rhythm. Just like Lon.

She exhaled, letting her tension go, and when Lon took his next breath, she did, too, matching her breathing to his, matching his steady rhythm.

To be steady and strong like Lon.

With his heart thudding beneath her ear, they danced a slow dance like that very first dance in the Elmhurst gymnasium. She felt fourteen again. Shy, inexperienced, painfully excited. The way his body touched hers…the way his chest brushed hers…the way his thigh moved between her legs…the way his fingers explored the hollow of her spine, she felt as if she were losing control.

No, she smiled against his shoulder.

She'd already lost control. She'd happily handed it over to him.

"So what do you want to do?" he asked.

Lightly she ran her hand across his chest, feeling the dark crisp hair curling on his chest, tracing the hair as it tapered down to disappear beneath the waistband of his pajama pants.

"It's up to you."

"Well, I'm up, but what we do is entirely your decision."

"And if I don't want…?"

His shoulders shifted. "We dance. We drink champagne. Or we do nothing."

"And if I want...?" she whispered huskily.

"We do."

"Without even knowing what I want?"

She felt his smile. "I'm sure I'd enjoy just about anything with you."

She wasn't so sure. "I could be a lousy lay, you know."

"A what?"

"A lousy lay."

He tensed, muscles rippling in his flat abdomen. "I was teasing. I shouldn't have—"

"You don't know. You've never had sex with me."

He lifted his head, looked down at her, his blue eyes burning. "You always call it sex, don't you?"

"It's the term," she said awkwardly.

"It is if you're with a stranger. But we're not strangers. What's wrong with calling it lovemaking? Or making love?"

"It's never...felt like...love before. It's felt like... duty." She touched her tongue to her upper lip, her mouth too dry. "Marriage."

"Ah. No wonder you hate marriage."

"I don't hate marriage, I hate lies. I hate the loss of power, I hate that men get to go off and do what they want and women are expected to stay home and do as they're told—"

Alonso covered her mouth with his, silencing her. He kissed her until her head spun and her lips trembled and her body felt hot and electric everywhere. After a long moment he lifted his head.

"You'll never have that life with me," he said softly. "Now I repeat, what do you want?"

Her eyes locked with his. She drew in deep ragged breaths, her pulse pounding, her heart racing. She felt as if she were sinking faster and faster, drowning in his blazing blue eyes. "You," she whispered at last.

"Is there a certain part you have in mind?"

"No. I want—everything."

He wouldn't let her undress. He wanted to first kiss her like this, wearing her white lace wedding gown.

Lon sat down on the edge of the bed and drew her onto his lap. With his long arms, he could reach her ankles, and slowly, deliberately slid his hands up from her ankles, to her calves, over her knees to the inside of her thighs.

She trembled when his palms were halfway up her thighs and bucked when his hands came together, meeting at the apex where she was warm, oh so warm, and so very ready for him.

"Nothing fancy," she choked, as his fingers slipped beneath her lacy white panty.

He laughed softly against the side of her neck and lightly, teasingly outlined the hot silky shape of her.

"Lon—"

"This isn't fancy." He dipped a finger into her body where she was warmer, wetter, and traced her yet again.

"*Lon.*"

"We're not even close to Harvey Nichols." He'd found the sensitized bud with his wet, slick fingertip and the sensation of his finger stroking the delicate skin was almost overwhelming. Sophie wrapped her arms around Lon's neck and took his mouth with hers.

"Kiss me," she whispered, frantic, tugging at the string in his pajama pants. "Make love to me. Now."

"Untie the string," he said, and after she'd loosened the string, he stood and the silky pants fell from his hips.

He set her on her feet. "Now my dress," she insisted.

"Not quite yet." Instead he reached up beneath her dress, and tugged the panties down, lifting her right foot and then her left, freeing them.

He sighed, a deep husky sigh in the back of his throat as he reached up beneath her dress again, cupping the smooth rounded flesh of her bottom in his hands.

She loved the feel of his hands on her, loved where his bare leg and her bare leg touched, and when he sat down again, she moved back onto his lap.

"I want to sit on you," she whispered into his ear. "All the way." She'd never been on top in her life, but she was so curious about everything, so interested in just being with Lon, and she let him help guide her down on him.

Sophie gasped as he began to fill her.

He'd felt her tense, and he stroked her hips, the curve of her backside. "It's okay," he said. "Your body just needs time. Trust me."

"I do."

"Then kiss me."

She bent her head to his, and as she kissed him, he sucked her lower lip into his mouth and the sucking sensation made her whimper, her body tightening, clenching, and he thrust up into her and it was all she could do to not cry out.

He felt amazing inside her, hard and hot and yet, gentle, too.

She'd always thought of his big body as strong, tough, forceful. And yes, his body was strong and tough, as well as being very hard in certain places, but he didn't take her fast. He wasn't hurried. He was incredibly tender…controlled…and he lifted her, up and down, slowly, very slowly creating a tantalizing friction, but Sophie wanted more skin, closer contact.

"Can we please take this dress off now?" she whispered against his mouth.

"Definitely." He lifted her off him, and turned her around, undid the zipper and peeled the white lace dress from her shoulders, over her hips, to the ground.

Lon stretched her out beneath him on the bed, and kissed her as his body filled her, moving in and out of her as if time had stopped and there was nothing but them. With each deep slow thrust, the heat grew, fire building on fire.

For Sophie, the fire was something kinetic, shimmering through her, beating through her, making her hotter on the inside, making him harder, thicker inside her. As he grew bigger, her body gripped his, the sensation electric, exquisite, and she couldn't grip him tight enough, couldn't hold him long enough, couldn't contain the pleasure for as long as she needed.

It was delicious. It was maddening. Her body was a river of feeling, nerves and skin, emotions and mind, her head filled with pictures of the night and the sound of the falls, of the warm humid rain and the birds calling to each other again and again.

Sophie wanted him to stay like this with her forever. She arched against him, wrapped her arms around his neck. She wanted more of him. She wanted all of him. She wanted him inside her as deep as possible.

"More," she whispered, her body lifting, surging, shivering beneath his. She'd never felt so much and it was, she thought, just the tip of the iceberg, so to speak.

"You're smiling." He kissed her, his lips parting hers, his tongue stroking the inside of her cheek and she shimmied beneath him yet again.

"I like this."

"Surprised, aren't you?"

She loved how he could tease her now, despite all this, despite the fire and the heat and the intense melting sensation as he drew himself from her and then slowly, slowly entered her again.

She'd never had an orgasm before, but she was going to have one now.

Her body rippled, tensed, clenched. She struggled to hold him inside of her and yet he couldn't be contained and when he withdrew she sighed, and then sighed deeper as he slowly filled her again, this time her body tightening in waves of liquid warmth.

She was going to break.

She was going to shatter into a thousand pieces—

He was moving faster, his body surging deeper, and she felt the muscles in his biceps tighten.

She was reaching the point of no return and for a moment she grew afraid—she couldn't do this, couldn't let go, couldn't—and then she saw him, felt him, realized this was Lon, he was still moving, his hard features a study of concentration, his lashes thickly black and curved against his prominent cheekbones.

She'd never seen anyone so beautiful, or sensual.

And lifting her lips to his, she kissed him, deeply, passionately, drinking in his fire. She was rising higher and higher, the seductive friction of his skin making her feel a vortex of everything—sex, love, sex, love—and then she was spiking in and out of her body, a deep unending ride that started on the inside and shook her to the core. She wasn't alone, either. Alonso's body was rippling with life inside her, and they were both reaching for a pleasure she'd never known, had no idea even existed until now.

Until now.

Later, dreamy, sated, she curled against him, her body

warm and damp. She might be soft, curvy, but he was hard, tough, sinewy. How perfect.

"You know what you're doing," she murmured, still breathless, her body still sinfully weak, every muscle and nerve useless.

He lifted his head. Held her face, and kissed her. "Only with you, *carida.*"

Hours later, half asleep, Sophie felt Lon reach for her and it was the most natural thing in the world to move into his arms. They made love again and afterward, lying across his chest, she caressed the warm bands of muscle shaping his ribs. "Tell me something," she said.

"What's that?"

"How did Clive get mixed up with Federico and this Valdez guy?"

Lon's fingers tangled in her hair. "Money. As you know, Clive had gotten into trouble financially. He gambled on the stock market and lost. Scared, he dipped into Louisa's personal account."

And he lost it, too, Sophie silently concluded, getting far more of the picture than she wanted, even as she remembered the months where Clive didn't come home from work until late, remembered him terse, angry, almost despairing. He'd wake sick to his stomach. He'd return from work sick at heart.

No wonder. "Why didn't Louisa know?"

"Clive found another way to settle some of his debts."

"Federico," she murmured.

Lon nodded. "Clive had no idea what he was getting into."

"When did he realize?"

Lon shrugged uncomfortably. "Probably at the end."

At the end. What a horrible, dreadful phrase. The end. And said like that, there was no hope, no resolution, no peaceful conclusion. The end. The opposite of the beginning. The absence of optimism.

"Who told him?" she whispered, chilled. She felt Lon tense, his warm muscles hardening.

"I did."

Pictures of that night filled her head. They were ugly pictures, violent pictures and she shuddered, wondering how Lon could stand it. "Was that the same time you discovered his feelings for you?"

"Yes."

He said nothing else and Sophie realized he wouldn't. He'd been through hell that night in Sao Paulo, too. Not just physically, but emotionally, mentally, spiritually. Losing Clive would haunt Alonso forever. It was a nightmare he couldn't escape and he couldn't discuss.

Gently she touched his cheek. "I love you."

He placed his hand over hers, holding her palm to his cheek. "You know I need you, don't you?"

Her heart ached. "I'm just sorry it took me this long to understand."

"Better late than never," he answered, drawing her even closer against him.

In the morning, Sophie woke up alone. The drapes were still drawn but the air conditioner hummed quietly. It must already be getting hot outside, she thought, yawning and stretching.

After showering, Sophie wrapped herself in Lon's silk robe still lying on the floor by the bed. With the robe tied at her waist, she headed to the kitchen to see if she couldn't get a cup of tea to take back to bed.

She heard voices coming from the dining room. Flip was talking. "You're sure about the helicopter? Once we use it, we've left ourselves exposed."

"It's the fastest way to get her out of here," Lon answered curtly.

"Yeah, and the fastest way for you to get blown to bits," Flip retorted.

Stunned, Sophie pressed herself closer to the wall. They were talking about her, about sending her away, and Lon staying behind. "I won't get blown to bits," Lon said. "That's too easy for Valdez. He wants face time." He laughed but the laugh sent shivers racing down Sophie's spine. Lon didn't sound amused. He sounded cold. Detached. Clinical.

The third man, an Australian, spoke. "We're not going to just leave you here, mate. If you want to be croc food you can always come to Queensland."

"I don't have a choice." There was a note of finality in Lon's voice. "Father Perez needs to leave soon. I promised him he'd be back for the Christmas Eve Mass. I want you both on the helicopter with Sophie—"

"I'm not leaving you here alone," Flip interrupted. "You hired me for a job. I'm going to finish my job. We can split up. I stay with you. Turk stays with Sophie."

"I can do that," Turk agreed. "I'll make sure she reaches your family in Buenos Aires. She'll be safe with me."

Chairs scraped. The men were moving. "Helicopter leaves in twenty," Lon reminded. "I'll go get Sophie."

He didn't have to go far. He stepped from the dining room and saw her standing there.

Lon caught up with her before she reached her room. He wrapped a hand around her upper arm and turned her, even as he moved forward, pressing her against the wall. "Look at me."

She couldn't. He was sending her away. Lon was putting her on a helicopter with the priest and an Australian commando and he was staying here.

Staying behind.

She shivered as his hands braced on either side of her shoulders. "Do you think this is easy for me?" he demanded. "Do you think I like what's happening?

She balled her hands into fists. "You can leave. You don't have to stay. You don't have to do this."

"But I do. This is my job—"

"It's *not* your job. You own an emerald mine, and you export—"

"Sophie, we've wanted Valdez a long, long time. And he's here." Lon's tone turned flinty. "And he wants me."

"Which is why you should *run.*"

He smiled. Very slightly. "I don't run."

She snorted. "And you wonder why it took you so long to get a wife."

His eyes glinted a moment and his small smile faded. "If I don't stay and deal with this now, I'll be hiding and worrying my whole life. I don't want to hide. I don't want to worry about those I love. And look, how did Valdez get to me this time?"

Sophie swallowed. Through her.

She closed her eyes, shook her head. "You had no right to marry me. You had no right to do that to me—"

"I had every right! If something happens to me at least you're protected. You'll be named my beneficiary."

She gripped his shirt, dragged her face toward his. "Your *beneficiary?* Is that the best you can offer me? One day of marriage and you comfort me with money?" She released his shirt, ducked out from beneath his arm. "Let me go. I'm ready. I didn't bring anything with me. I'm not taking anything out."

He reached for her. *"Sophie."*

She spun away from him. "No! You can't ask me to be happy about this. I did not marry you last night to be widowed today!"

"It won't be today."

She covered her face, fought for control. She couldn't do this, couldn't love him and lose him, and be expected to play along. This wasn't supposed to happen. She'd been given the world last night. It couldn't be snatched away now.

Lifting her head, she looked up at him, tears swimming in her eyes. "Why does Valdez want you so bad?"

Lon reached out to wipe one of the tears clinging to her lashes. "I killed his brother."

She sniffed, lifted her chin. "Tell me more."

He studied her for a long moment. Deliberating. He sighed. "I was there that last night in Sao Paulo. I was there the night Clive died."

Sophie bit her lower lip so hard she drew blood.

Flip appeared at the end of the hall, motioned to Lon. Sophie saw Flip but Lon didn't move. Neither did she.

"What happened that night?" she demanded.

"There was a trap set for undercover agents—narcs waging a war against Valdez' cocaine empire—Valdez disposed of them, very painfully, and very slowly, and not wanting any witnesses, he disposed of Clive, too."

"How do you know this?"

"I was one of the narcs." Lon closed his eyes, pain creasing his features. "By some miracle I didn't die. But I witnessed what atrocities took place that night, and I'm the only man still alive who can put Valdez at the scene—and get a conviction."

"So why hasn't he gotten to you before?" The edge had gone from her voice. She just felt tired now. Tired, and scared. Lon was going to stay.

"I'm *really* good."

He'd tried to be funny, tried to keep it light, but she couldn't muster a smile for him. She stared at him, studying him.

He was so macho male. So incredibly protective of her. He'd been like this forever. She certainly wasn't going to change him now. All she could do was love him. And pray he'd return to her in one piece.

Sophie rose up on her toes and kissed him, her hands pressed to his chest, and then reluctantly pulled away. "You better be."

"Throw some jeans on. We'll have to hurry."

Sophie found jeans and a lavender blue knit top in the dresser. She didn't have much choice in footwear and put the boots back on.

Lon took her hand as she left the bedroom. "It's going to be okay."

She looked at him, expression somber. "Not if you don't come home to me."

CHAPTER TWELVE

WITH her fingers curled in his, he led her through the house, and then downstairs. But instead of walking toward the river and the dock, they headed the opposite direction, toward the back of the property. The rain forest seemed to press insistently on all sides, masking the intimidating iron fence protecting the perimeter of the estate.

They were walking toward what looked like a large garage constructed of concrete and steel tucked into thickets of green bamboo and palm trees. The garage roof—what she could see of it—was steel, too, but painted shades of green.

Camouflage, she thought, and her stomach dropped, as she realized that this was all real. Nervously she wiped her damp palms on the sides of her black jeans. She was really leaving. Alonso was really staying.

Lon tangled his fingers in her hair, lifted her face to his. "I've been in far worse situations, Sophie."

His blue eyes were even more intense in daylight. She reached up, touched his cheek, tracing the faint white scar. "How'd you get this?"

His lips curved. Emotion burned in his eyes. "The night I took down Valdez' brother."

She stared at him incredulously. "What kind of life have you led?"

He caught her fingers, carried them to his mouth. "A tough one, but it's had incredible rewards." Then he smiled, and the sadness in his eyes cleared like a wind sweeping the blue sky clean. "You're my reward. You have to know I'm not losing you now, not after everything we've been through.''

The side walls of the garage slid open and the enormous steel roof parted. The whole building was unfolding like a flower. Sophie's eyes widened at the helicopter inside.

Lon walked her to the helipad. The helicopter's rotors were already turning.

She felt the pressure created by the spinning blades, and the wind that tore at her hair and shirt. ''When will I see you?'' she pleaded, balking at the door.

He lifted her up, into the helicopter. ''In Buenos Aires.''

Inside, as Turk moved forward to secure the door, Sophie leaned out, reaching for Lon. ''Not where, when?'' she shouted, the noise incredible.

''Have faith in me.'' Then Lon shut the door, stepped back, and the helicopter lifted straight up into the air.

I do, she whispered, pressing against the glass to get a last glimpse of him. But the helicopter was rising too swiftly, already the ground looked impossibly far away. Alonso had vanished. And looking down, Sophie saw only a sea of green. The steel green roof had shut.

Turk took her arm. ''Let's get you buckled in,'' he said, steering her toward the back.

She stumbled into a seat, across from Father Perez. The elderly man leaned forward and patted her hands. ''Have faith,'' he said and eyes watering, she nodded.

Faith, she silently repeated, concentrating on buckling the seat belt, which wasn't easy when her hands shook so badly.

Sophie forced her attention to landscape in miniature below. The sun was rising higher, the soft greens brightening as the gold morning gave way to the intense heat of day. Faith. The same word Lon had used.

*   *   *

They were starting their descent. Again.

An hour and a half ago they'd dropped Father Perez off in Posadas, south of the falls, and then immediately taken off, heading for Buenos Aires on the coast.

Now they were descending fast. The nose of the helicopter seemed to be tipping down and looking out her window, Sophie saw the enormous sprawl of a big, cosmopolitan city.

The helicopter landed on a pad in the middle of the city. Turk immediately moved forward, unlocked the inside of the door and stepped out to speak to the man waiting for them on the helicopter pad.

The man was dressed in all black—black shirt, black slacks, black belt and shoes—and with his arms crossed and sunglasses on, he looked like the devil himself.

Finally Turk returned to the helicopter and opened the door. "Come on, sweetheart. You're okay."

She didn't feel okay. Sophie exhaled slowly, blowing a tendril of hair from her eyes. She felt tired, frazzled, *frantic*.

It was all getting to be a bit much for her. Too much drama, too much worry, too much tension.

This is exactly the kind of thing she'd wanted to avoid. Her parents' world had been full of drama and tension. She didn't want it for herself.

Turk looked at her questioningly. "Do you want me to stay with you?"

That would be silly. She knew Turk was needed somewhere else. She'd prefer him to return to Iguazu and provide some much needed backup support for Flip and Alonso.

Gathering her courage, Sophie walked toward the big, unsmiling man dressed in black.

"Hello," she said awkwardly, pressing her damp palms to the sides of her jeans. "I'm Sophie."

He uncrossed his arms, held a hand out. "Lazaro Herrera." And his upper lip curved in a hard, cool smile. "One of Alonso's half brothers."

She shook his hand, rather awed. Alonso was big but Lazaro was even taller. And harsher. *"One?"* she asked huskily, her voice failing her.

Lazaro shrugged, and pulling off his sunglasses, a smile flickered in his dark eyes. "It's quite a family."

She could believe that, if this was a sample of what was to come. "Are they…all…like you?"

He laughed softly and harsh lines in his face eased. For a moment he looked young, and a lot like Alonso. "Oh no, I'm the nice one."

Her jaw dropped and she made a soft choking sound. Lazaro laughed again before sliding his sunglasses back on. "Actually, I'm here because I'm the one no one likes to mess with." But he didn't seem to mind his reputation. "Come, let me take you to Dante's house. The rest of the family's gathered for Christmas and they're eager to meet you. Especially Anabella."

Sophie recognized the name. "Alonso found her baby."

"That's the one."

They took the elevator down to the street level. A black limousine waited. Lazaro helped her into the back of the limousine and then joined her.

Twenty minutes later they pulled up in front of a tall elegant house in Recoleta, one of Buenos Aires' oldest, wealthiest neighborhoods. The sun shimmered on the creamy beige stone walls and the trim topiary trees flanking the door were festooned with gold and white ribbon.

Lazaro didn't wait for the driver to step around. He opened the door, and held out a hand to Sophie. Even before they'd reached the house's wrought iron gate, the front door opened and everyone spilled out—one girl, many little boys, two very blond women, another woman, and several men behind them.

Sophie took a step backward and bumped into Lazaro. He steadied her. "When I first met them, I felt the same way," he whispered in her ear.

But they were nice, she found, later as she sat down for lunch with them. Just as Lon had said. They weren't phony nice, but real, and the women were smart and funny, not to mention quite patient considering all the male arrogance dominating the room.

The children were allowed to leave the table when they'd finished and Anabella turned to Sophie. "You can't keep them still on a day like this. It's Christmas Eve. They're absolutely crazy." Her smile stretched as she watched her two boys race down the hall. "That's Tomás," she said, indicating the taller boy, "and Tulio, the little guy. He's almost five now. Hard to believe it's my third Christmas as a mother. What a difference a couple of years can make."

"So," Zoe leaned forward, a swaddled baby nestled against her breast. "Tell us about the wedding."

Daisy smiled. "In case you don't know, Zoe's the romantic." Daisy nodded toward the men arguing passionately at the end of the table. "She'd have to be. She fell in love with Lazaro."

Anabella joined in the good-natured laughter. "You can tell Daisy's the big sister," she chimed in. "Daisy has an opinion on everything. But she's usually right."

The maid announced that coffee and dessert were being served on the terrace and Daisy invited everyone to join her outside. And Sophie, who a moment ago, had been enjoying herself, found herself fighting tears.

Everybody was here. Eating and drinking, laughing and talking. Yet Alonso was in Iguazu—doing God knows what.

She turned from the terrace, stepped back into the house, hastily wiping her eyes. For all she knew he could be hurt already. Or...*dead.*

"He's a smart man," a deep male voice interrupted her morbid thoughts. "Very sharp."

Sophie looked up, blinking tears. The man was dark and tall like the others, but his nose was a little crooked, his cheekbones more chiseled and he wore his long hair in a ponytail. The gaucho, she thought. The one who'd married Anabella. "You're Lucio?"

He nodded, his expression grave, his dark eyes sober.

"It was your baby Alonso found," she said.

"He wasn't much of a baby when Alonso discovered him. He was five." Lucio's eyes narrowed. For a moment he was quiet and Sophie sensed that he struggled with the past, and the years that had been taken from them. Then his expression eased and Lucio shrugged. "But Alonso did find him, and when he came home to us, it was a miracle."

"You had your son back."

"We had two sons." Lucio's smile grew. "Tomás had adopted a little fellow at his last orphanage and when he came home with us, Tulio joined him. So you see, in Tomás' eyes, Alonso is a superhero. Uncle Alonso gave Tomás his mama and papa, and he gave little Tulio a family, too."

"A superhero?" she repeated softly.

"Sounds silly, but you know children."

She felt a prick of tenderness and pride. "Doesn't

sound silly at all. I've always teased Alonso that he's superhuman.'' She bit her lip, pictured that first night at the Langley-Elmshurst dance. ''I've known him practically forever. And I still call him Superman.''

''Then you know you can count on him.

She swallowed around the lump blocking her throat. ''I just wish he were here. It's—'' and she swallowed again, fighting fatigue, fighting tears ''—Christmas.''

''Almost,'' Lucio corrected gently. ''You still have a day.''

So she waited, trying to hide her fear, trying to keep a brave face. That night Sophie went to bed in the guest room, and woke to the shrieks of excited children on Christmas morning. Still no word, she thought, watching the children open their gifts, bright red and green paper torn, ribbon and tissue shredded everywhere. But the children were happy, and that was what Christmas was about.

Only Tomás, the handsome green-eyed little boy with gorgeous olive skin, looked up from his new computer game to ask, ''When is Uncle Alonso coming?''

The adults fell silent and for a moment no one spoke. Then Anabella took charge, answering cheerfully, ''Soon, Tomás. Your uncle would never forget us on Christmas.''

And Anabella turned, looked at Sophie, and smiled. Anabella's smile was fierce, tough, so much like Alonso's that Sophie's eyes burned. ''Alonso is a Galván.''

A Galván, Sophie silently repeated, but it was cold comfort as the afternoon slipped away and darkness descended.

Christmas was nearly over. It was well after ten o'clock and the children had finally been put to bed. Close to midnight the adults sat with glasses of wine in the living room, talking, always talking, and of all of them, it was Dante and Lazaro who talked the most. Mainly together, both their dark heads bent in deep and earnest conversation.

Sophie jumped when the hall clock chimed one. A half hour later she set her untouched wineglass on the table near her chair. In Argentina she knew it was fashionable to stay up very late, but Sophie was exhausted. Emotionally wrung out. Christmas was over without any word from Lon.

She should go to bed. Get some sleep. Sleep was the best thing at a time like this. But in the hall, instead of climbing the staircase, Sophie opened the front door and stepped outside, closing it softly behind her.

The night was still warm, and she slowly walked down the front steps, noticing for the first time that the house was protected from the street by elaborate gold-tipped wrought iron gates.

What would she do if Alonso didn't return?

Where would she go? Where would she live?

But she didn't want to think like that. Lon *would* come home. Lon said he'd come back for her.

And she knew him. She trusted him. Lon didn't make promises he didn't intend to keep.

The front door opened. Dante appeared in the yellow light of the doorway. "Would you like company?" he asked.

Of all the Galváns, Dante, the eldest was the most beautiful. He and Anabella were both movie star beautiful, but what Sophie liked about Dante was his intelligence and warmth. Like the others, he was proud, but his strength was tangible. As was his integrity.

Like her Alonso.

It's funny, she thought, but the Galváns weren't at all like she'd expected. The men might be aggressive in business—and they'd probably earned their reputation for being ruthless—but what was important to them was the family. Always the family. For this generation of Galváns, the women and *los niños* came first.

Dante moved down the steps. "Daisy and I have been talking, and we'd like to host a wedding reception for you and Alonso, when he returns. It doesn't seem right to be married into this family without some kind of celebration."

"Thank you." She smiled gratefully at him. "And thank you for saying, *when* Alonso returns, not *if.*"

Dante's gold eyes glowed warm. Kind. "I have no doubt he'll be back soon."

She felt a shiver race down her spine fueled by curiosity and adrenaline. "None?"

"None."

Down the street a car's headlamps flashed white, cutting a bright swath through the night.

Dante began climbing the stairs, back to the door of the house. "Keep your eyes peeled. You might just see Christmas yet."

Holding her breath, she watched the car's progress, hoping, praying. What if it were Alonso? What if he had come back to her? What if everything was really, truly all right?

Then the car slowed and did a U-turn in the middle of the street, heading back the direction it'd just come.

Sophie bit her lip. Silly to get her hopes up. Silly to think that out of the blue Alonso would just appear.

But when the car had turned the corner and started this way, and after Dante had sounded so sure of himself, so confident, as if he knew something she didn't, she'd gotten her hopes up a little.

She'd thought maybe, just for a moment, she'd thought…

"Sophie."

The quiet voice whispered through the night. She stiffened, goose bumps covering her skin and faced the street, eyes searching the dark street. A shape moved from the shadows. A big man, tall dark, incredibly imposing.

Her man.

She couldn't get to the gate fast enough. Her hands shook trying to open it. "What are you doing here? How did you get here?" she cried. "Why won't this gate open?"

"You are rather impatient, aren't you?" Alonso teased, finding the lock and twisting it open. He thrust the gate wide, and wrapping his arms around her, he held her tight. "Happy Christmas, *muñeca.*"

The front door flew open again. Galváns poured out. Lucio bounded down the stairs and swept Alonso into a gruff bear hug. Sophie blinked back tears as Lucio's big arms surrounded Lon, and he lifted him off his feet. There couldn't be a more sincere or loving greeting. And as Alonso's brothers and sisters surrounded him, welcoming him home, Sophie realized that Alonso was truly one of them. Truly a Galván. It wasn't just the family name, but it was the fire, the spirit…the pride.

Then like yesterday, it was again calamity in the house. The noise woke the children, and Tomás and Tulio were clinging to their uncle, giving him the same fierce warm hugs their father had given him, and Sophie's eyes burned all over again.

This is what she'd wanted all her life. Family. Brothers. Sisters.

Love.

Anabella wrapped her arm around Sophie's waist and dragged her into the kitchen with everyone else.

"So what happened?" Lucio demanded as Anabella

began pulling food from the refrigerator, making up a special Christmas plate for Alonso.

Dante moved closer. "Was there a confrontation?"

"And Valdez," Lazaro asked, dropping into a seat across the table from Alonso. "What of him? Was he captured? Did he get away?"

Sophie's head spun. The men were nearly as loud as the children, demanding details from Alonso. *What happened in Iguazu? What about Valdez's man, Federico Alvare? How many soliders did Valdez have with him?*

Seated at the massive kitchen table, Sophie on one side, the rest of the Galváns surrounding them, Lon recounted the confrontation with Valdez.

"Except it wasn't much of a confrontation," Lon concluded, "because the MI6, U.K.'s Secret Service had teamed up with the CIA and the Brazilian and Argentine's elite police. All the forces had already moved into the area, the safe house we were staying in was completely surrounded." He shook his head once, remembering. "Valdez and his men didn't stand a chance."

"So Valdez is in jail?" Lazaro persisted.

"He refused to be taken—at the last minute he turned his gun on himself," Alonso answered before glancing at the children, remembering they were there and breathlessly hanging on to every lurid detail. He tempered his tone. "There were high casualties on Valdez's side. Alvare died on the scene, as did Valdez, but that was his choice, not ours. Most of our boys came out fine."

"Ours?" Sophie repeated, not entirely sure she understood the reference. Just who was he referring to?

"Lon's department. The MI6." Anabella answered.

Sophie's eyes narrowed. She stared at her husband. "*Lon's* department?"

Eight-year-old Tomás nodded vigorously. "Uncle

Alonso's a spy. He works for Her Majesty. In *England*,"
he added importantly.

The children were all nodding now, chorusing, "*In
England*," making it seem the most exotic country on
earth.

Lon, a spy? The Secret Service? The MI6? They'd all
seen far too much James Bond. Sophie looked at Lon.
She wasn't sure if she should laugh or cry. "You're a
spy?"

Anabella and Lucio exchanged quick glances. Zoe
moved closer to Lazaro. The rest of the adults fell silent.

"You didn't know?" Tomás asked, incredulous.

Alonso cleared his throat. He reached for his water
glass, took a sip, set the glass down very carefully. "We
don't use the word spy anymore, *carida*. It's officer.
Sometimes operative."

Impossible. "You're a spy?"

"*Was* an officer in the MI6. I retired a couple years
ago. Two years ago." His eyes met hers, the blue depths
haunted. "I took a hard hit."

"How hard?"

"Lost my best friend."

Suddenly she understood, suddenly she saw what she'd
never quite pieced together before. Why Lon was there
that night in Sao Paulo, why he knew so much about the
details of Clive's life even though they'd stopped talking
years ago. Why Lon could do what he could do, and how
he had so many…interesting…connections.

She slipped her hand into his, leaned close to him, and
whispered, "I think you and me need some alone time,
darling."

Upstairs Lon shut the door and Sophie stood in the
middle of the room just looking at him. She shook her

head. Lon's jaw tightened. "I'm sorry I didn't tell you. I just couldn't—not while Valdez was alive—"

"I understand," she interrupted softly.

"You do?"

She nodded, and moved toward him, sliding her hands up his chest. "You didn't want me to have information that could get me hurt."

"It was better you not knowing, at least, not knowing the kind of danger I routinely put myself in."

She held her breath, searched his eyes. "Are you *really* retired?"

"I'm really retired. I'm just a boring old emerald mine owner these days."

She felt as if a horrible weight had fallen from her heart. She'd been so worried, so scared for him. But Lon was fine. *They* were going to be just fine. "That is dreadfully dull." She sighed, ran her nails down his chest. "I suppose you'll want to shower me with jewels."

"Jewels?"

She heard the husky laughter in his voice. "Yes, jewels," she answered, pressing a kiss to his lips. "Or, if you prefer, you can just overwhelm me with lots of you."

"Which part of me?"

She could feel which part he was thinking about, that part was most definitely interested in…discussion, but Sophie didn't want sex. She wanted love. To make love.

"All of you." She kissed him again, parting his lips with hers and giving him a tantalizing taste of her tongue. "If you don't mind, that is."

He didn't mind, and they made love with an almost desperate need.

He'd been so careful with her in Iguazu. Their lovemaking had been slow and gentle. Yet tonight Lon couldn't seem to get enough of her, and Sophie sensed he was trying to forget what had happened with Valdez, trying to forget the possibilities of how things could have turned out if the MI6 and CIA and local police hadn't been there.

She welcomed the rawness of his hunger, and he took her without restraint, touching, kissing, licking, tasting, and it all felt right between them.

She'd finally accepted his intensity.

He'd finally accepted she wouldn't break.

And when he drove into her, his hard body almost relentless in its demands, he gave her freedom. No limits, she thought, and no more hiding.

Later, Sophie curled closer to Lon in bed, her hand on his big chest. "If I had to spend Christmas without you," she murmured sleepily, "I'm glad I spent it with your family."

He slowly kissed her, lingering over her tender lower lip. "You like big families, don't you?"

"Mmm. We could have saved ourselves a lot of trouble if you'd only pulled out these Galváns ten years ago."

His chest rumbled with laughter. "That's all it would have taken to win you? A couple of brothers and sisters?"

"It certainly would have helped." She flashed a naughty smile. "They're all gorgeous. Each one of them, although I kind of think the bad one, Lazaro, is my favorite—"

"Excuse me. You better think carefully on that."

She giggled and slid across him, her hips gliding teasingly over his, and she was immediately rewarded with a hard response.

"*You're* my favorite," she whispered, kissing his cheek and then his mouth, loving the smell of his skin, loving the hard textures and rough planes. "You're one tough superhero, you know that, Alonso Galván?"

He kissed her back, incredibly tenderly for a man with his strength. "I've heard. I believe it runs in the genes."

The world's bestselling romance series.

HARLEQUIN®
Presents~

Seduction and Passion Guaranteed!

Miranda Lee...
Emma Darcy...
Helen Bianchin...
Lindsay Armstrong...

Some of our bestselling writers are Australians!

Look out for their novels about the Wonder of Down Under—where spirited women win the hearts of Australia's most eligible men.

THE AUSTRALIANS

Don't miss
The Billionaire's Contract Bride
by **Carol Marinelli**, #2372
On sale in January 2004

Pick up a Harlequin Presents® novel and you will enter a world of spine-tingling passion and provocative, tantalizing romance!

Available wherever Harlequin books are sold.

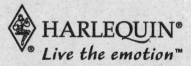

HARLEQUIN®
Live the emotion™

Visit us at www.eHarlequin.com

HPAUSJ04

If you enjoyed what you just read,
then we've got an offer you can't resist!

Take 2 bestselling
love stories FREE!
Plus get a FREE surprise gift!

Clip this page and mail it to Harlequin Reader Service®

IN U.S.A.
3010 Walden Ave.
P.O. Box 1867
Buffalo, N.Y. 14240-1867

IN CANADA
P.O. Box 609
Fort Erie, Ontario
L2A 5X3

YES! Please send me 2 free Harlequin Presents® novels and my free surprise gift. After receiving them, if I don't wish to receive anymore, I can return the shipping statement marked cancel. If I don't cancel, I will receive 6 brand-new novels every month, before they're available in stores! In the U.S.A., bill me at the bargain price of $3.57 plus 25¢ shipping & handling per book and applicable sales tax, if any*. In Canada, bill me at the bargain price of $4.24 plus 25¢ shipping & handling per book and applicable taxes**. That's the complete price and a savings of at least 10% off the cover prices—what a great deal! I understand that accepting the 2 free books and gift places me under no obligation ever to buy any books. I can always return a shipment and cancel at any time. Even if I never buy another book from Harlequin, the 2 free books and gift are mine to keep forever.

106 HDN DNTZ
306 HDN DNT2

Name	(PLEASE PRINT)	
Address	Apt.#	
City	State/Prov.	Zip/Postal Code

* Terms and prices subject to change without notice. Sales tax applicable in N.Y.
** Canadian residents will be charged applicable provincial taxes and GST.
  All orders subject to approval. Offer limited to one per household and not valid to current Harlequin Presents® subscribers.
® are registered trademarks of Harlequin Enterprises Limited.

PRES02   ©2001 Harlequin Enterprises Limited

The world's bestselling romance series.

HARLEQUIN®
Presents
Seduction and Passion Guaranteed!

A gripping, sexy new trilogy from

Miranda Lee

THREE RICH MEN...

*Three Australian billionaires—they can have anything,
anyone...except three beautiful women....*

Meet Charles, Rico and Ali, three incredibly wealthy friends all
living in Sydney, Australia. Up until now, no single woman has
ever managed to pin down the elusive, exclusive and eminently
eligible bachelors. But that's about to change, when they fall
for three gorgeous girls....

But will these three rich men marry for love—
or are they desired for their money...?

Find out in Harlequin Presents®

A RICH MAN'S REVENGE—Charles's story
#2349 October 2003

MISTRESS FOR A MONTH—Rico's story
#2361 December 2003

SOLD TO THE SHEIKH—Ali's story
#2374 February 2004

Available wherever Harlequin® books are sold

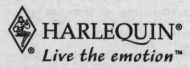

HARLEQUIN®
Live the emotion™

Visit us at www.eHarlequin.com

HSR3RM2

The world's bestselling romance series.

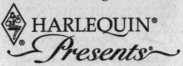

Seduction and Passion Guaranteed!

They're guaranteed to raise your pulse!

Meet the most eligible medical men of the world, in a new series of stories, by popular authors, that will make your heart race!

Whether they're saving lives or dealing with desire, our doctors have got bedside manners that send temperatures soaring....

Coming in Harlequin Presents in 2003:

THE DOCTOR'S SECRET CHILD by Catherine Spencer
#2311, on sale March

THE PASSION TREATMENT by Kim Lawrence
#2330, on sale June

THE DOCTOR'S RUNAWAY BRIDE by Sarah Morgan
#2366, on sale December

Pick up a Harlequin Presents® novel and you will enter a world of spine-tingling passion and provocative, tantalizing romance!
Available wherever Harlequin books are sold.

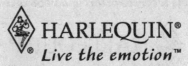

Live the emotion™

Visit us at www.eHarlequin.com

HPINTDOC

Season's Greetings from

HARLEQUIN®
Presents

Seduction and Passion Guaranteed!

Treat yourself to a gift this Christmas!

We've got three Christmas stories
guaranteed to cheer your holidays!

On sale December 2003

THE YULETIDE
ENGAGEMENT
by
Carole Mortimer
#2364

THE CHRISTMAS
BABY'S GIFT
by
Kate Walker
#2365

THE DOCTOR'S
RUNAWAY BRIDE
by
Sarah Morgan
#2366

Available wherever Harlequin books are sold.

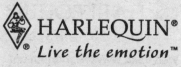

HARLEQUIN®
Live the emotion™

Visit us at www.eHarlequin.com

HPXMAS03

eHARLEQUIN.com

The eHarlequin.com online community is *the* place to share opinions, thoughts and feelings!

- Joining the community is easy, fun and **FREE!**

- Connect with **other romance fans** on our message boards.

- Meet your **favorite authors** without leaving home!

- **Share opinions** on books, movies, celebrities…and *more!*

Here's what our members say:

"I love the friendly and helpful atmosphere filled with support and humor."
—Texanna (eHarlequin.com member)

"Is this the place for me, or what? There is nothing I love more than 'talking' books, especially with fellow readers who are reading the same ones I am."
—Jo Ann (eHarlequin.com member)

**Join today by visiting
www.eHarlequin.com!**

INTCOMM

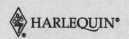

INTRIGUE

Nestled deep in the Cascade Mountains of Oregon, the close-knit community of Timber Falls is visited by evil. Could one of their own be lurking in the shadows...?

B.J. Daniels

takes you on a journey to the remote Northwest in a new series of books far removed from the fancy big city. Here, folks are down-to-earth, but some have a tendency toward trouble when the rainy season comes...and it's about to start pouring!

Look for

MOUNTAIN SHERIFF
December 2003

and

DAY OF RECKONING
March 2004

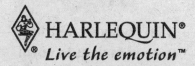

Live the emotion™

Visit us at www.eHarlequin.com

HICQMS